Haunted Island

Haunted Island

True Ghost Stories from Martha's Vineyard

Holly Mascott Nadler

Illustrations by Liza Coogan

DOWN EAST BOOKS

Text copyright © 1994 by Holly Mascott Nadler
Illustrations © 1994 by Liza Coogan
ISBN 0-89272-353-X
Library of Congress Catalog Card Number 94-72609
Book design: Eugenie Seidenberg Delaney
Cover photograph: Alison Shaw
Color separation: Roxmont Graphics / High Resolution
Printing and binding: Capital City Press, Montpelier,Vt.

9 8 7 6 5 4 3 2 1

Down East Books / Camden, Maine

For my boys,
Marty and Charlie

Acknowledgments

I OWE A SPECIAL DEBT OF GRATITUDE to Eulalie Regan, indefatigable librarian of the Vineyard Gazette archives. Without the archives, historical research of Martha's Vineyard would be not only incomplete, but impossible.

Also thanks to the Dukes County Historical Society for its fascinating materials.

So many people placed me on the track of so many good stories. Of particular helpfulness were the following: Barbara Nevin, Everett Whorton, Gail Stevenson, Mark Luce, Dr. Dean Lusted, Lynda Hathaway, Jimmy LeBarre, Donald Widdis, Karen Coffey, Daron Wright, Will Holtham, Eulalie Regan, Virginia Poole, Jerry Averill, Judy Federowicz, Emma Carmichael, and Laurie Bradway Lickteig. All others interviewed for their direct experiences with ghostly phenomena are credited in the chapters. I was impressed by the number of interviewees—definitely the majority—who allowed me to use their real names.

Contents

Foreword

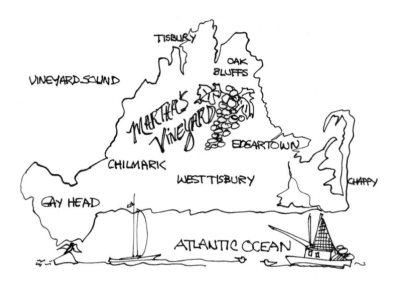

I MIGHT NEVER HAVE BELIEVED IN GHOSTS had I not encountered a couple of them myself. The first cropped up shortly after my dearest friend in college, Jane Thompson of Estes Park, Colorado, died in a car crash. I kept Jane's memory alive by imagining her spirit to be with me at all times. One of the ways I symbolized her nearness was to leave record albums playing for her in my old apartment in Pasadena, California, even after I'd rushed off to class. One day I realized I never bothered to place on the turntable any music of special interest to Jane. Searching my memory, I recalled her love of James Taylor's *Sweet Baby James* album, particularly the song "Fire and Rain," and determined to play it for her when I got home.

That evening, my resolve forgotten, I stacked up the following recordings instead: Vivaldi's *The Four Seasons,* a collection of piano rags by Scott Joplin, and an old album of Linda Ronstadt's from back in the days when she sang with The Stone Ponies. Skipping down the hall accompanied by Vivaldi's strings, I filled the bathtub and submerged myself for a good long soak all through the Italian settecento and Edwardian ragtime. It wasn't until the pause between Scott Joplin and Linda Ronstadt that I remembered with a wince my pledge to air my late friend's favorite album.

The silence ended, and from the living room a lonely guitar reverberated as a silken male voice crooned, "Just yesterday morning, they let me know you were gone." Not only was it the James Taylor album, but the right side and the exact song!

Later, considerably shaken, I examined the album jackets to make certain I hadn't unconsciously pulled the James Taylor album from my collection after all. But no, the gold and white Stone Ponies jacket rested beside the stereo, along with the plain yellow Vivaldi cover and the green and brown Scott Joplin cover. Even though the James Taylor album rested on the turntable, its blue and gray jacket was nowhere to be found.

The other ghost introduced itself in a dusty, cobwebbed room in the Big Sur Inn on the Monterey coastline. My mother and I had stopped there for the night, and in total darkness between twin beds lodged against opposite walls, we heard the unmistakable sounds of a man loudly snoring. The next morning we mentioned this odd feature of our stay to the inn's owner, an eccentric young man with a long name succeeded by the numeral IX. "Oh, that was Grandpa," he said blandly. "He must have liked you. If he doesn't care for the people staying in the room, he scares them away in the middle of the night. Several times I've had to ship guests' bags on to the next town."

Whether or not one believes in ghosts, there's a tendency to be titillated by a seemingly authentic tale of occult doings. I adore a good ghost story, provided it's related to me during the bright light of day. Come nightfall, if the account remains fresh in my mind, I'm suddenly afraid to wander downstairs to lock the door and turn off the lights. I don't know how many people are as skittish as I am, but let's hope the following stories won't lead to too many derailments of the bedtime routine.

I arrived at a desire to write about the ghosts of Martha's Vineyard by a circuitous route. After residing on the island for eleven years, I decided to put together my own series of walking tours. They had to mix equal parts entertainment with history, and I immediately thought of the wonderful walkabouts in London with subjects ranging from "Favorite Pubs of the Bloomsbury Circle" to "Follow in the Footsteps of Jack the Ripper" to, you guessed it, "The Ghosts of London."

For my own ghost tour, I chose 350-year-old Edgartown, that bastion of whaling captains' derring-do, of eighteenth-century gentlewomen with English airs, of passions and family secrets and all the vices of a sailors' port. I simply knew that the minute I began to make inquiries, the stories would pour in, and indeed they did. Sometimes the customers on my walks would turn the tables and tell me hair-raising tales of their own.

In time I became known as "the ghost lady" (an amusing but not altogether comfortable sobriquet), and people began to contact me with supernatural accounts from all over the island. For Edgartown alone cannot contain all the island's spirits. Restless souls also ramble over the moors of Gay Head and Chilmark, pervade the manor houses in the dark woods of West Tisbury, and haunt the hallowed Campground and long-ago Victorian saloons and bordellos of Oak Bluffs.

I decided to write about them.

Most of the stories told to me I've believed, especially when people of obvious sobriety and substance in the community relate them to me. I pride myself on possessing an inbred "baloney-meter," so when intuition whispers to me that someone is possibly molding the facts to suit some personal thrill or delusion, I simply nod politely and go on to the next one.

Some of the ghost stories in this anthology scare me, some make me thoughtful, some even make me laugh. I genuinely hope they'll provoke the same reactions in you.

Holly Mascott Nadler
Martha's Vineyard Island

1

The Return of Desire

IN THE NINETEENTH CENTURY they called her Desire.
Not Desiree, but Desire as in the dictionary meaning: "conscious impulse toward something which
promises enjoyment in its attainment."

Descended from the aristocratic Coffin family of Nantucket, in the mid-nineteenth century Desire married Captain John Osborne, an Edgartown master mariner, and
moved into his commodious house overlooking the harbor on North Water Street. Not one to pine for her man
from the vantage of a widow's walk, it was rumored about
town—and even written up in the local news—that Desire

Coffin Osborne had a secret lover. Her other passion was music. Desire imported the first piano to Edgartown and she spent hours poring over favorite parlor pieces by Lizst, Chopin, and other popular composers of the day.

Not too many years ago, Anthony and Diane Bongiorno of Connecticut rented the house on North Water Street for the summer. They knew nothing about Desire Coffin Osborne other than the fact that from the second-floor landing, Desire's likeness seemed to scrutinize them. If the alleged adulteress with the seductive name had once been beautiful, the painting gave no hint of it, other than a warm probing quality to the subject's velvet-brown eyes. Mrs. Bongiorno, a collector of art, believes the ocher tints on the antique canvas had deepened and bled into Desire's face, giving her a somewhat sinister and formidable air. She remarked, "My three children, who were very young at the time, were frightened by the portrait. There was a hotel-type bell stationed on a small table beneath the painting, and they used to ring it when they ran past, as a way of warding off harm."

The Bongiornos rented the house every summer for several years without anything out of the ordinary taking place. Mrs. Bongiorno loved the old home with its bevy of gracious chambers, such as the ornate dining room with a fireplace at each end; every room stocked with charming antiques. The only missing element was a piano. Like Desire, Mrs. Bongiorno loved to play, but the original instrument had long ago been donated to the Dukes County Historical Society. She rectified the situation by purchasing a baby grand for the front parlor.

One summer morning, an elderly neighbor named Mrs. Bliss, a descendant of Desire Coffin Osborne's, stopped by with her nephew, a talented pianist and composer named Ned Barto. Ned, although on vacation, wondered if he could spend a couple of daily hours at the Bongiorno piano finessing his new composition. Mrs. Bongiorno cordially agreed, and for the next few days the occupants of the house on North Water Street enjoyed the rich sounds of Ned's playing.

One day Ned appeared with a dusty treasure under his arm. In his aunt's attic he'd come across a leatherbound folio of nineteenth-century parlor music. On the cover, inscribed in gold gilt was the name: Desire Coffin Osborne. Ned had retrieved his ancestress's personal collection of piano pieces. Jointly excited, he and Mrs. Bongiorno set a date for his return to perform Desire's music.

It was a jasmine-scented August evening and all the windows of the captain's house stood open to the sultry breeze. Ned began to play an elaborate sonata of Chopin's and, seated on surrounding chairs and divans, the Bongiornos were captivated both by the beauty of the music and the extraordinary power and depth of Ned's musicianship.

Out on the sidewalk, a crowd collected. Soon acquaintances and strangers alike pushed into the foyer and outer sitting rooms until the house and garden swelled with rapt listeners. For more than two hours, Ned's performance of Desire's favorite pieces electrified the ever growing throngs and floated out over the moonlit harbor, and, somewhere far beyond the mortal coil of human activity, it seemingly transcended this world and summoned forth a denizen from the next.

Shortly after two o'clock in the morning, every member of the household—parents, children, and nanny—bolted awake at a loud creaking on the stairs. Unnerved by the unmistakable sounds of an intruder, all six souls congregated on the third-floor landing. The sounds of footsteps ceased, but now everyone watched in utter shock as the door to a neglected wing opened and closed by some invisible hand.

The same disturbance occurred every night for the rest of the summer, invariably between two and three o'clock in the morning. The timing of the sudden haunting, following upon the heels of Ned's concert, convinced the Bongiornos that Desire Coffin Osborne had returned to her house in an obsessive search for something. Her music? Her lover? Both?

Another ghostly manifestation troubled the household: At least once a week, without the slightest provocation, the fire alarm would shrilly blare. On each occasion, one of the town's finest electricians, John Farrar (who uncannily shows up in several of our stories), would arrive at the house and spend a long time dismantling and tinkering with the wiring. He would leave scratching his head: nothing appeared to be wrong with the system.

Presently Ned returned to the mainland. At the end of the summer the Bongiornos also left North Water Street. The house, which had never been fully winterized, was closed up for the winter. If on frigid nights, amid covered furnishings and dark walls, with the fog horn tolling from the Sound and the only illumination twinkling coldly from the moon, the stars, and the Edgartown Light, if on these stark occasions Desire still roamed her house, no living soul exists to speak of it.

The following summer, the Bongiornos once again took possession of the harborfront home. Obviously their adjustment to the ghost from the previous summer allowed them to return without a shred of apprehension. Sure enough, from the very first night, the same eerie disturbances occurred. Everyone, including the home's resident ghost, was present and accounted for.

Ned Barto also reappeared but he was disquietingly altered. Paler and thinner than before, he was easily fatigued. He continued to pay daily visits to play the piano but he seemed distracted. More and more he set aside his own work to occupy himself with Desire's folio of music and, on summer afternoons, the sumptuous sounds of Lizst and Chopin would waft across the rose gardens and the wharves of the Edgartown harbor. Other times Ned would disappear upstairs, only to be found staring with thoughtful absorption at the portrait of Desire Coffin Osborne.

At the end of the summer, Ned's aunt, Mrs. Bliss, quietly informed the Bongiornos that the brilliant pianist had been diagnosed with leukemia. The following winter, at home in Connecticut, Mrs. Bongiorno received the news that Ned Barto had died.

In the succeeding summer, the family returned to their house on North Water Street anticipating a reunion with the ghost. The first night transpired without incident. So did the second and third nights. In fact, nothing disturbed the household for the remainder of the summer. Desire had fled. In the words of Mrs. Bongiorno, "Her absence was so total, it made her previous presence in the house all the more real."

The ghost's arrival directly after Ned Barto's concert, and its disappearance following the composer's death, planted a firm belief in Mrs. Bongiorno's mind that the events were inextricably linked. One can only speculate about the relationship between Desire and Ned. Was the connection purely familial or perhaps, to romanticize, were they lovers in another life—specifically in Desire's life— and was it the music that reunited them across the bridge of time? On a darker note, was it possible that Desire, reawakened by Ned's impassioned plea across the piano keys, drew him to her? And had Ned, on some unconscious level, as he played the temptress's pieces and gazed at her velvet-brown eyes and ocher-stained face, accepted her summons?

We will, of course, never know. Today's house on North Water Street (cared for by the Society for the Preservation of New England Antiquities) lies once again empty in the winter and cozily occupied in the summer. Desire Coffin Osborne's portrait still stares from the second-floor landing, but the folio of piano pieces has disappeared.

2

The Secret Staircase

I T'S ODD HOW INHABITANTS OF THE SPIRIT WORLD exercise such good taste in their choice of hotels. Generally they seem to haunt the best-appointed, most charming ones; you never hear about "the ghost of the U-Turn Motel." A case in point is The Daggett House on North Water Street in Edgartown (North and South Water streets being two of the most ghost-packed lanes in New England). Since 1948, when the Chirgwin family extended its holdings and bought the seventeenth-century establishment, the haunting of The Daggett House has amazed staff and guests alike.

In 1984, a new manager, Daniel O'Connor, had heard stories about the ghost, but, like most people who pride themselves on a stern scientific approach to life, O'Connor had refused to lend credence to the rumors. Early in the spring before he opened the doors for business, the innkeeper spent his first night alone in the hotel. As he prepared for bed in his room on the third floor, he heard the distinct sounds of footsteps mounting the stairs, then the unmistakable tread of someone ambling down the corridor. Whoever it was stopped directly outside O'Connor's room. The manager froze as three hollow knocks thudded against his door. (In the annals of New England superstition, three knocks "tolled for thee" signifies that the Grim Reaper has arrived as your personal escort to the Back of Beyond.) In O'Connor's case, the dull raps seemed to have represented a simple mysterious greeting, for when he opened the door he found himself staring into an empty hallway. The new manager was hastily converted into a believer of ghosts.

Over the years other employees have reported odd encounters. Sometimes, after one of the maids has methodically made up a fresh bed and has momentarily left the room, she'll return to a pile of disheveled sheets, blankets, and spreads, as if a child had entered the room and, in one mischievous swoop, had undone all her careful work. Other times one of the staff will hear his or her name called out from the next room but, upon investigation, will find no one else on the floor. But the bulk of the hauntings seems to emanate from the ancient chimney and the secret stairwell mounting the building alongside of it. . . .

In the early 1660s when the first white men and women cleared away the Indian relics and built their dwellings along the harbor, a small cottage went up on the site of The Daggett House. In 1751, Captain Thomas Pease expanded the building, adding the Colonial beehive fireplace. Stocking locally distilled beer and the rum and aqua vitae freely circulated by sailing ships gliding up from St. Kitts, Barbados, and Jamaica, Captain Pease established one of the most popular taverns in the New World. We can only imagine the boisterous, boozy voices, the tall tales of skirmishes between pirate ships and British men-of-war, the illegal but nonetheless popular games of cards, and the air fetid with the smoke of homegrown tobacco. Then, in 1801, Captain Timothy Daggett bought the pub and converted it back into a home. Yet something must have transpired in this time frame of history, or perhaps later in the nineteenth century, to create one of the most enduring spirits in Vineyard lore.

Some say that one of the many whaling captains to occupy the home locked his children in the room (now known as Room Eight) above what was once the tavern. Another tale places a young bride in the barricaded chamber as a means of preserving her chastity during the three or four years of her husband's post-honeymoon whaling voyage. The room itself evokes a melodrama from a Nathaniel Hawthorne novel. You approach it from downstairs through a tavern door (now part of the dining room) disguised as a column of bookshelves. Once you've found and unlocked the secret latch, you enter a tunnel of small, wooden, eighteenth-century steps curving up to still another door—small and cribbed like a pre-Revolutionary closet—and a second set of stairs.

The room, with its antiques and thick carpet and view through small-paned windows to the harbor, emits the subtle air of Daggett House luxury. It's a bower ideal for romantic trysts, and yet on occasion something else—something from another world—seems to touch down here, although, oddly enough, the event is usually experienced by someone outside the chamber.

The hotel staff have reported the sound of a child's weeping coming from Room Eight, but every time someone has mounted the steps to investigate, he or she has found no occupant to explain the sad distraction. Other guests in the adjoining room have mentioned being awakened in the night by a child's desolate wail issuing from the other side of the wall, only to learn no child currently occupied the chamber above the ancient fireplace.

The eeriest story about Room Eight concerns a traveler from Bermuda who reserved the bower for a summer weekend. On a Saturday night, he traversed the dining room, opened the secret door, and ascended the stairs. He was never seen again. Even his luggage disappeared.

"We think there's probably a plausible explanation for it," chuckles John Chirgwin, Daggett House co-owner (with his brother, Fred). "Maybe he'd been traveling light and met some friends at a bar who talked him into a boat cruise. But it struck a nerve that he hailed from Bermuda. You had to wonder if he simply got sucked into the vortex of the Triangle!"

Sometimes the ghost invades other rooms. One night the pilot of a private jet checked into a front room on the second floor. He lay in bed watching a television, which had been tastefully recessed in an antique cabinet. At 11:00 P.M., just as the network news program loudly trumpeted its first breaking story, the television switched off and the doors of the cabinet swung firmly shut. "I couldn't believe it!" he reported later. "It was as if an invisible presence was telling me it was time to go to bed!" In the morning, his alarm rang at six o'clock, even though he'd set it for seven-thirty. Instantaneously, the cabinet doors swung open and the television flicked on again. Later at breakfast, the flight attendant who had occupied the room next to his, swooped angrily down at his table and cried, "That was a crummy joke you played on me, setting my alarm for six o'clock!" She refused to believe him when he protested his innocence, blaming the incident on the ghost.

The most lasting impression of something supernatural existing in The Daggett House derives from a photograph taken a few years ago. A crew of shutterbugs visiting from New York snapped some pictures of the inn. They were drawn particularly, as is everyone, to the 250-year-old dining room with its low beams, sloping wood floors, thick windowpanes, and antique Windsor chairs. Someone took a photograph of logs toasting in the beehive fireplace. Later, in the darkroom, a strange image materialized in the flames: In the crux of two whitish burning logs, the face of a young boy had expressed itself.

An enlarged version of the now-famous photograph hangs at the inn, a curiosity for guest and passerby alike. And, for those who know the stories, we can't help but wonder if this is the spirit who periodically invades The Daggett House, tousling bedclothes, calling out names, or, when events of the distant past overwhelm it, bewailing some long-ago tragedy late into the night. Maybe one day this ghost will find a more coherent way to tell us what ancient sorrow keeps him trapped inside the walls of this seaside hotel.

3

The Sad-Eyed Lady of Hariph's Creek

I F THIS APPARITION HAD APPEARED in the hills of Sardinia or the south of France, people would have undoubtedly felt they had beheld the Virgin Mary. An entire cult might have sprung up around the sightings. Instead, it appeared on mysterious moonlit nights in the wilds of Chilmark, and for years the three ladies who saw it breathed not a word to anyone, not even to each other.

The house that Irene Allis leases from one of the island's oldest dynastic families was built in 1972 over a site once dear to the Wampanoag tribe. In fact, when the excavation began for the foundation, the workers found Native American artifacts and the midden of an ancient habitat. The Indian name for the area was Nashowaquidsee— "nashowa" meaning divided or doubled and "aquiden" meaning islet.

Bridge House sits on a rise overlooking the spot where Quitsa Pond meets Stonewall Pond at a juncture called Hariph's Creek. With a huge hunting lodge–style living room, well-appointed bedrooms, and stunning water views to the north, west, and south, it's no wonder famous people have rented the house in the high season—among them Vernon Jordan who, in the summer of 1993 hosted a birthday party for President Bill Clinton, on the veranda.

But it was during the cold of February 1980 that longtime leasee Irene Allis entertained the spirit. At Bridge House, Irene had been suffering from an increasingly debilitating flu. All along she had contemplated driving the seventeen miles down-island to see a doctor, but she soon realized she'd grown too weak to drive anywhere. Irene moved from the spacious master bedroom, which faced north overlooking Quitsa Pond, to the smaller, cozier chamber called the Blue Room. "The Blue Room is a cheerful room," she told me later. "We only call it blue because of the print on the white wallpaper." Situated above Stonewall Pond and the ocean to the south, and therefore protected from the harsh north winds, the Blue Room seemed to beckon to Irene with its promise of succor.

"One night my fever broke," she recalled, "and I had to get up a couple of times to change the sheets and my nightgown. When I finally returned to bed, I was very restless. I was tossing and turning, and, when I looked toward the door, I saw the figure of a woman. With the light of the moon shining through the window, she seemed to blend into the wallpaper. She was tall and thin and she had straight, dark hair. She stood very still. I didn't see her move. I wasn't in the least bit afraid. I thought she was there because I was so sick. Her presence was comforting. I dismissed her from my thoughts for years. Seeing a ghost was not something I could tell anyone. They would think I was a crackpot."

Irene spends much of her time in La Jolla, California, and when she's away her good friend Elizabeth Carroll often journeys down from Cambridge to enjoy some private time in Bridge House. In the autumn of 1984, Elizabeth also found herself alone in the house, ensconced in the Blue Room, and possessed of a severely troubled state of mind. "I had suffered a loss—a death in the family—and was unable to sleep comfortably. I tossed and turned, and dozed off and on. At one point I looked up and saw a woman standing in the doorway. She was about five-foot-nine. Her hair was long—it seemed to be pulled back. I think she had silver in it. She was elegant, slender, with very square shoulders. She held her hands stretched in front of her, in a pose of reaching out to me. She never moved. I'm quite sure she could have moved, but she stayed perfectly still. My sense was that she wore something blue and green, something that seemed to be made of feathers. The outfit looked ceremonial. The moon really is quite bright when it comes in the window of the Blue Room, and it gave her a shimmering effect, or maybe she shimmered naturally."

Elizabeth thought that the woman's exotic appearance might suggest she was a Wampanoag of an earlier period. What most impressed Elizabeth was that the apparition actually made eye contact with her; she seemed to be aware that Elizabeth was aware of *her*. "I felt that she had understood sorrow and troubled times and was there as a support.

She was different than a human being; she wasn't made of fluids and skin. There was something spectral about her—as if she visited from another dimension—but she wasn't frightening or threatening. At the time I saw her, I kind of shook my head disbelievingly—after all, I was a math major in school and firmly based in reality. Then, when I looked again, she was gone. Yet even as I tell the story, there's a certainty that I saw something. In a way she's still with me."

Like Irene, Elizabeth kept her experience to herself, imagining her grief had projected her into a state of delirium which created this particular hallucination. It wasn't until another three years had elapsed and a third woman was visited by the compassionate phantom of Hariph's Creek that Irene and Elizabeth's encounters came to light.

Elizabeth explained, "A woman named Rita was here, a houseguest from Texas, and, in the morning, as we sat in the living room, she casually announced, 'Y'all know y'all have a ghost in this house?' I thought someone was playing a joke until I remembered I'd never told anyone about what I'd seen. Irene came running out of her bedroom and we all three started madly talking about it."

Rita was recovering from a devastating love affair.

All three friends realized that sorrow was what drew the woman to the same vigil in the doorway. As Elizabeth related the story to me, she was reminded of a folk song of the 1960s written by Leonard Cohen: "That one about Suzanne taking you down to the river. There's a verse in there about Jesus, that only drowning men can see Him. That's how it was with the sad-eyed woman. She glimmered on that spot in our time of need."

Elizabeth's remark reminded me of another Leonard Cohen ballad that eerily evoked the quality of the apparitions. In "The Sisters of Mercy" mysterious spirits of the night materialize at one's bedside to comfort and heal with a grace and love as natural as the greening of spring.

Elizabeth reflected that though she's frequently alone at Bridge House and walks across the apparition's hallowed ground in the doorway all the time, she's never frightened. "I'd like to see her again, but I never have," she told me.

"Well, good! You haven't been sad enough!" I replied. We chuckled that Irene might consider renting the Blue Room to those in need of solace.

So who is this figure from the past whose own perhaps unexorcised grief draws her back to this place to provide comfort, even healing, for the living? If the apparition's own tragedy carved a ghostly path for herself, then the area's history, in this century alone, provides some ready candidates. There was the highly regarded Nanetta Madison (1883–1973), wife of Napoleon Madison, whose Medicine Man's Lodge burned down in December 1956, destroying her files of old legends and the prized leather costume she wore when lecturing about the history of the Wampanoag tribe. Or we might consider Mrs. Hattie Diamond (1900–1948), whose house caught fire in July 1935, extinguishing the lives of two of her three children. Or Mrs. Ann Judson Madison Foster (1835–1933), another native and life-long dweller of Gay Head, whose first husband was lost on a whaling voyage, and whose second husband sustained a permanent injury during a fishing expedition on the chronically cruel sea. Ann had attracted some renown as a storyteller, her tales spiced with anecdotes both humorous and grim. In summer a collection of eager listeners would seat themselves on the broad step outside her house while Anne, shaded in her doorway, entertained them with her verbal repertoire.

But there's also the tantalizing notion that the spectral figure goes further back in time to an age before the depredations of the white man, when Wampanoag braves canoed from Stonewall and Quitsa ponds to larger Menemsha Pond to the north, and a beautiful, compassionate woman watched from the crest of the shore, a sheath of healing herbs in one hand, a wave for her brethren raising the other.

4

"Old Joe" of the Jail

I T'S HARD TO IMAGINE a more cynical group of men than police officers, and yet for several decades the staff at the Edgartown Hall of Corrections has freely attested to the regular appearances of a ghost. It's equally hard to believe that in this white-clapboard, black-shuttered house, with its picket fence and overall air of "Leave It To Beaver" wholesomeness, anything unpleasant could ever transpire. But back in the early 1950s, an inmate jailed on a drunk and disorderly charge hanged himself in his cell. Many of the officers believe the hauntings date from that incident. To protect the sensibilities of the family of the deceased, many of whom still reside in Edgartown, the prison staff clapped the nickname "Old Joe" on the jailhouse spirit.

Old Joe comes and goes, but when he visits he generally announces himself with a cold zone at the top of the stairs leading to the cellblock. Says Sergeant Randy Ditson, who has worked the night shift for over a decade, "People complain that in the winter we overheat the building. The furnace runs continuously and every room feels like an oven. But then, some nights when you climb the stairs, you hit this freezing section and you know Old Joe is back."

Old Joe calls attention to himself by turning on faucets, the radio, and overhead lights. A favorite activity is pecking away at the typewriter keys. "We're always hearing unidentified typing," reports Sergeant Ditson, "but we can turn the office and cellblock upside down and never find the source of the noise."

Years ago a young man was arrested for sleeping on the dunes at South Beach. The only soul to be incarcerated that night, he was kept awake until dawn by the sounds of typing. "I couldn't figure it out," he revealed years later. "If the only crime committed on a Saturday night in July was sleeping on the beach, then how the heck could the cops have so many reports to type up?" On the morning following his arrest, he mentioned this conundrum to the guard reporting for duty. The officer stared blankly at him. "No reports were typed up last night," he responded with a shrug. Nearly a quarter of a century later, when the former miscreant returned to the island as a middle-aged citizen, he learned that the jail was haunted. He came to the conclusion that the well-known specter had been responsible for his sleepless night.

Old Joe also announces his presence with mysterious footsteps. One night Officer William L. Searle sat at the typewriter with his back to the door. He heard the tread of footsteps in the corridor overhead, then the telltale creak of someone descending the stairs. The footsteps proceeded down the hallway, paused outside Searle's office, then entered and crossed to the desk. Searle turned to see which of the other guards had come to talk to him, certain that the sounds of approach placed the visitor squarely at his back. No one stood anywhere in the room with him.

The ghost has sometimes materialized as a visible presence. Downstairs at the command center, eight video monitors enable the officers to track everything going on inside or outside of the jail. For a period of time, during every graveyard shift between two-thirty and three o'clock in the morning, the outside camera would track an indistinct fuzzy white shape on the sidewalk. Without fail, the transparent blob would turn in at the gate, gravitate up the walk, and disappear into the building. Many of the guards have seen a blurry white entity flit across one of the screens, but Officer Eric Perry was surprised one night to see on one of the monitors the silhouette of a man seated at the top of the stairs outside the cellblock. Wondering how one of the inmates could have wandered outside the locked gate, Perry charged up the stairs to apprehend the figure in the shadows. When he reached the landing, he found only an empty chair and all the prisoners securely sheltered in their cells.

The most dramatic sighting occurred a few years ago when a young woman was brought in screaming hysterically. Although uncertain about what had triggered the outbreak, the arresting officers knew that the prisoner was in a highly charged emotional state as, interspersed with her incoherent shrieks, she expressed a wish to commit suicide.

Placing the girl in the observation chamber downstairs, they huddled in the office to discuss the appropriate way to help her. Through the walls, her screams raged out at them.

Suddenly, Sergeant Ditson, stationed at the far end of the downstairs hall, beheld a funnel of white sweep in from the opposite end of the corridor. Like the scouring tornado of an old television commercial, the furious white cylinder whirled down the hallway and passed through the thick door of the young woman's cell. Her shrieks abruptly ceased. Later, peering through the one-way glass, the officers ascertained that the prisoner looked calm and tranquil, as if no outburst had attended her arrival in the jail. She remained peaceful for the rest of the night, and when questioned in the morning about her sudden change of mood, she had no recollection of ever having suffered a bad one. In this scenario Old Joe appears as a most benevolent spirit.

The hauntings at the tiny prison have, on one occasion only, carried an element of sinister intent. Sergeant Jerry Jeffers once crossed the room where the monitors are housed and felt a sudden bump on his shinbone, as if an invisible joker had tripped him. Down he fell, with no sight of an offending carpet or jagged floorboard to explain the accident.

Aside from this one act of malice, Old Joe seems quite helpful. He apparently gave one inmate winning tips about the state lottery. On a work-release program, the prisoner would leave the jail and return that night with windfalls of various sizes. One time the prison staff was forced to rescind the man's day outside his cell. He insisted the ghost had bestowed on him a hot number and urged the officers to play it themselves. They did so, only to discover the ghost's tip was indeed the winning number. In New York.

Oddly enough, this inmate appeared to have devel-

oped a closer association with the spirit than anyone before him. He claimed an apparition often appeared to him
dressed in a sailor suit and walking a ghostly dog. The
guards discredited his statements until one day the inmate
mentioned the ghost's real name, the one the staff had re-
ligiously suppressed to protect the family. "How do you
know his name?" snapped Sergeant Ditson. "He told me,"
the inmate replied with a shrug.

Some of the more senior officers insist the jail has been
haunted even longer than Old Joe's chronology would indicate. Sheriff Christopher Look heard ghost stories about
the building when he was a young man learning the ropes
from Fred H. Worden, who was master and keeper of the
jail prior to World War II. In 1901, another prisoner, it
turns out, had also committed suicide inside those sturdy
walls. A theory has stayed afloat for some time that this
earlier tragedy created an atmosphere for the first incidence
of jailhouse hauntings.

Built in 1848, the jail's foundation was constructed
of granite stones carted by wagon from West Tisbury, having been purloined from land held sacred to the Native
American population around an area called Christiantown.
It's not impossible that these transplanted rocks created an
environment hospitable to lost souls. Certainly this motif of
violated Indian property, both real and personal, crops up
repeatedly in tales of Vineyard ghosts. All of Edgartown itself, arguably the most paranormally disturbed of all the
island villages, was once, according to many Wampanoags,
the site of an ancient cemetery, with myriad burial mounds
grouped along the shore. Today, North and South Water
Streets, which meander along the harborfront, contain a
harrowing amount of haunted houses.

Folklore-steeped Vineyarders of Wampanoag extraction insist these prehistoric tombs were plundered by the first white settlers who, coming upon bones and relics in the laying of their foundations, would crassly chuck the remains on the nearest refuse pile. Although the conclusions drawn from these allegations sound absurdly like the premise of a pulp thriller, too many echoes of this theme arise on the island to allow us to totally discount the notion.

So how does this theory affect the quaint village of Edgartown, with its elegant Greek Revival façades of white clapboard, its aubergine-black shutters and its summer gardens of every blossom known to New England? Well, if there's anything to it, these picturesque byways are doomed to suffer disturbances of a supernatural nature as long as the white man remains entrenched here, which is to say forever.

As far as the jail is concerned, the guards on the night shift have reported no ghostly sightings for over a year. But the visits come in cycles, so any day now, whether in the hectic pace of summer or in the somnolent stretch of winter when rain and wind assail the eaves, Old Joe of the jail could reappear to switch on spigots or radios or to tap someone on the shoulder. Whatever his schedule, he seems to have drawn a life—and death—sentence.

5

Possession of the Demonic Kind

OR REASONS THAT WILL BECOME OBVIOUS, the identity and location of this house must remain a secret. Suffice it to say that it nestles in one of the island's numerous seaside colonies of mostly summer homes. Rather grand in design, it sits on a rise of several acres. Gray shingles, blue trim, and an eye-catching assortment of windows, some of them vaguely Gothic, lend the house a unique character. In contrast to the well-maintained grounds and façade, the interior of the home is shabby and neglected; a result of the unhappy presence that haunts the rooms, driving long-term inhabitants away.

Unless it first drives them mad.

An island woman, Caitlin McAuley,* recalled having skittish feelings about the house when as a young girl she summered in a cottage down the road. "I was never a fearful kind of child," she said. "The dark never bothered me. I didn't scream when people said 'Boo!' But every time I had to walk past that house—and this had never happened to me before, and hasn't happened to me since—the hairs on the back of my neck would stand on end. It spooked me so much that I finally learned to avoid that stretch of the road."

As the years went by, Caitlin was never surprised to hear about the terrible events that took place in the house. She remarked, "Other people noticed it, too. It seemed as if there were some sort of dark spirit there just waiting to pounce, and if someone who was weak moved in, this 'thing' would just push him over the edge."

One summer a quiet man lived in the gray-shingled house without drawing any particular attention to himself. Then one day he seized a kitchen knife, opened the back door, and stalked across the grounds. He arrived at a nearby cottage where a group of college-aged women shared a summer rental. He plunged into the room with the upraised knife and attacked the first young woman in his path. The others grabbed at any blunt object that came to hand and sprang on him, knocking him to the ground. Within minutes he was arrested and hauled to jail. Later, the stunned roommates questioned what might have happened if they hadn't rallied themselves to resist him: Could he have ma-

---

*Names changed to protect confidentiality.

terialized into another Richard Speck, the depraved killer who had, years before in Chicago, bound and systematically murdered some young nurses?

A few years later another strange event occurred when a group of young singles rented the house for the season. As the summer wore on, one of the young men in the party grew increasingly morose. Occupying a bedroom on the second floor, he kept to himself with his door closed. But every so often his roommates could hear the slow shuffle and thud of furniture being moved in his room. Through the recluse's momentarily opened door, one of his peers glimpsed what looked like the formation of a highway of furniture leading to the window. When the last piece was positioned in place, the young man walked down the path of chairs, bed, desk, and bureau, and leapt out the window. He survived the fall but was taken into custody for psychiatric treatment.

Even animals appear to be adversely affected by the evil presence pervading the house. A few summers ago, a year-round family, who lived nearby, strolled the maze of winding roads with their elderly pooch. As they rounded the wooded lot of the house in question, a hostile Rottweiler sprang from the yard. Snarling and barking, he attacked the older, smaller dog as if the latter had not only invaded his territory but had also stolen his favorite bone. Shrieking, the family managed to tear their pet away, but a portion of his hide flapped bloodily from his neck. The family rushed their pet for emergency stitches from their veterinarian. Since that day, even without their dog in tow, the family has strictly avoided that entire section of woods.

Finally, Caitlin, the young woman who as a child had bristled whenever she passed the house, found her own inchoate fears at last presented with pure fact. Her sister,

Fiona,* fell in love with a young man who had recently arrived on the island. Fiona knew little about her new boyfriend, other than that he seemed friendly, warm, and responsible. She signed a lease with him to rent the gray-shingled house for the winter.

After a short while the young man developed a drinking problem—something Fiona swore he'd shown no signs of before they'd moved in together. He proved to be a nasty drunk and in no time began to assault her. On a couple of occasions the police had been summoned and the disorderly man had been arrested. At last Fiona moved out. Alone in the house, her lover killed himself.

To this day the woman involved in the tragic love affair blames herself for her lack of perception: How could she have failed to see from the start that the young man must have housed a battleground of private demons? But Caitlin knows better: "It was that 'thing' in the house. My sister's boyfriend might have been a little unstable to begin with, but it was that 'thing' that pushed him over the edge."

From where does this malignant presence hail? The house is only fifty or sixty years old, and in its early days, nothing untoward took place there. Perhaps, then, the answer lies in the area itself—a wooded enclave along a curving shore with a Byzantine system of winding paths and roads where even long-time residents easily lose their way. Many centuries ago Native Americans quartered there in the summer when cool, fragrant breezes swept in from the Sound. Later the area was rife with smugglers and mooncussers; brigands who on dark nights used illusory lighthouse flares to guide sailboats to treacherous shoals, enabling these land pirates to pillage from the wreck whatever valuables floated to shore. These murderous thieves found the hidden coves perfect for their nefarious work.

Then, in the early 1940s, a lurid homicide took place in a large establishment on the nearby bluffs. The crime was never solved, though the police found suspects aplenty.

Do these past influences have any connection with the disturbances in the gray-shingled manor house? Only God knows . . . and, perhaps, the sinister presence that lives and breathes in its walls.

6

Guardian Angel

LIKE SO MANY YOUNG COUPLES starting out in life, Ginny and Pete Alden* had little money and few assets. But living on Martha's Vineyard, as they had for several years, they found they were rich in resources. Pete, in particular, having summered on the island all through his childhood, found himself surrounded by helping hands. A case in point: An old friend offered him and his family an Edgartown winter residence free of charge in return for light caretaking responsibilities.

The two-story home on North Summer Street had belonged to the friend's grandmother who had died of natural causes some years before. The kindly woman, descended from one of the island's original seventeenth-century families, had shone in Pete's earliest memories as a dream grandma. Smiling serenely, Grandma Nora* would dispense cookies to a flock of neighborhood children while simultaneously bandaging a bruised knee or administering a kiss to a momentarily neglected toddler. But Pete's most vivid recollection—and his most distressing—involved an August afternoon in his ninth summer when he and his friend had been bicycling on North Summer Street. A small pickup truck had rounded the corner from Morse Street and his friend had been struck from the rear, his small body sent hurtling twenty feet to land with a sickening thud on a nearby lawn.

Grandma Nora had hovered beside the hospital bed until her grandson had achieved a full recovery. Other family members had put in their time, too, but it was the older woman whom Pete recalled had exhibited the greatest devotion; something about her smile, her touch, her very presence, had seemed to convey a sort of mystical healing.

Grandma Nora might have died, but her memory lived on in the quaint house with its antique furnishings and family portraits. The problem was that the house had never been properly winterized. Lacking storm windows, only panes of thin glass faced gusts of Arctic air flowing in from the harbor. On frosty nights, the old heating system wheezed and groaned as it exhaled tepid blasts of air through time-worn registers.

Ginny and Pete decided, therefore, to situate themselves downstairs where the warmth from the kitchen per-

*Names changed to protect confidentiality

meated the living room and ground-floor bedroom. Their two-year-old son slept in a snug alcove alongside the pantry and, in the kitchen, the cozy effusions of heat from the old-fashioned gas stove incubated their five-month-old infant in his cradle.

But something was going on upstairs, in the rooms never visited. At night Ginny and Pete would lie awake listening to footsteps treading from room to room. Doors opened and closed. It sounded as if, over and over, someone was making a systematic search of the entire second floor. The first time they heard it, the couple suspected an intruder had entered through an upstairs window. But almost immediately they realized a cat burglar—or whatever it was—would take greater pains to be quiet, especially with lights blazing downstairs in the tenanted portion of the house. After a while they decided the even creak of footsteps overhead represented the methodical vigil of the home's late mistress. "It's Grandma Nora," they would chuckle, as they went about their business, just as the spirit upstairs seemed intent on going about its.

"I think she likes us here," commented Ginny one evening over supper in the warm kitchen. All through the winter the young mother had felt as if her little family had been immersed in an overall atmosphere of good will. When she returned from the grocer's on a cold winter evening, her infant in her arms and her toddler in a stroller, the lamps from the front windows would cast a welcoming amber glow along the walkway. But it was more than the soft lights, and the soup on the stove, and the fruity potpourri on the mantle: a benevolent mood seemed to permeate the household.

"Of course she likes us," replied Pete. "Grandma Nora always told me I was one of her favorites."

"But she doesn't have to like your bride," teased Ginny.

"Obviously she does," he grinned back at her.

One night the couple prepared for bed in the usual manner: Pete went about checking the windows, making sure they were closed against the raw air—not that the slightly warped old windows with their rusted hinges were in any danger of easing open, but, all the same, the young man enjoyed the ritual of locking up for the night. Ginny bedded the baby down in the cradle and adjusted their sleepy toddler in his narrow bed with its complement of stuffed animals. She switched off the lights and tiptoed to bed.

The family dozed.

A couple of hours later the young man and woman jerked awake simultaneously. They bolted upright from the pillows, staring at one another with absolute clarity. "We felt as though we had drunk a thermos of coffee!" Ginny reported later. "That's how awake we were!" To their absolute astonishment, they saw that the window facing them stood wide open to the dark night.

Without another thought, they raced from the room. In the hallway, another window gaped open, admitting frigid drafts of winter air. The couple flew to their toddler's alcove to find his window, too, had been opened wide. Ginny snatched the sleeping child from his bed and scurried after her husband into the kitchen. Above the long trestle table, another open window admitted a column of cold air from the garden. The baby nestled in his cradle, but from the interior wall accommodating the stove, a nasty odor reamed the room: gas.

Pete pulled out a drawer and grabbed the biggest wrench he could find. He threw open the kitchen door and pounded in bare feet over the icy lawn. When he reached the fuel tank, he twisted the valve to stop the flow of gas to the house.

Returning, he found Ginny on the steps outside the kitchen, a child in each arm, both baby and toddler weeping with their rude awakening. Yet the young couple were overjoyed to find they'd all been spared asphyxiation in their sleep.

"At first we thought the draft from the strangely opened windows had blown out the pilot light," said Ginny years later. "But when the repairman examined the stove, he found the line itself had developed a malfunction. We knew then that Grandma Nora—or whoever the ghost was who haunted the upstairs—had come down in the night to make us wake up. She—or it—opened a window in each room to let in air so the baby wouldn't die before we could get to him. She saved all four of us that night and I think of her to this day as a guardian angel."

The charming old house on North Summer Street has since been winterized and its old gas stove has been replaced by a modern electric range. But whatever lucky family dwells there now must occasionally be aware of a friendly spirit hovering over the house like a shimmering genie in a fairy tale.

7

The Ghosts of Winter

Those ancient summer houses hump
like elephants along the shore
each a grotesque amorphous lump
for fourscore weathered years and more.
—Barbara Greenough Bradley

AFTER KIM ANGELL'S PARENTS bought their waterfront manor in 1966, the young girl had the impression that unseen presences performed baby-sitting duties for her and her siblings. "West Chop is such a social community, and my mother and father attended a lot of cocktail parties. They felt safe leaving us, and we felt safe being left," she explained.

From the very beginning, the twenty-five-room summer "cottage" had appeared to the Angell family to be amply stocked with guardian spirits. In the off-season, however, whenever someone attempted to inhabit the house, the atmosphere underwent a radical change. The ghosts seemed to get testier, if not downright cranky. Kim reported, "I don't know if the spirits simply believed winter was *their* time, or if the cold weather made them edgy, or if a whole new set of ghosts moved in." A sort of otherworld version of a winter rental?

Kim's mother, Carol Angell, initially skeptical of any talk of ghosts in her seaside manse, spent several days alone there one long-ago September. One night she awoke with an intense sensation of someone watching her. Opening her eyes, she beheld three females in diaphanous white gowns standing at the foot of her bed. She had the unshakable impression that they were the daughters of the original owners; Beacon Hill debutantes, most likely.

On another occasion when Mrs. Angell remained behind past the season, when traces of sepia and rose veined the privet hedge along the cliffs, she stepped out onto her second-floor balcony only to hear a voice in her ear announce, "It's time to go, Carol."

One October, a young shipbuilder rented a room at the Angell manor, never thinking he might feel uneasy being alone in so large a house. As he settled into bed one night in a downstairs room gently heated by a Kero-Sun burner, he heard a door slam shut overhead. Mystified, he climbed the stairs to investigate, found no draft to explain the disruption, and so returned to bed, only to hear another door slam shut. Again he journeyed upstairs and this time methodically closed each and every door communicating off the long hallway. The minute he returned to his bed and rested his cheek on the pillow, he jerked convulsively as *bang! bang! bang!* an endless succession of doors overhead opened and slammed shut.

Another time, in April, Kim's brother and a college friend spent the weekend in the house. As they sat in the kitchen enjoying a midnight snack and chat, they glanced up simultaneously and beheld an apparition: On the far side of the window, through which dishes and cutlery could be passed into the pantry, a man and a woman gazed stonily at them. With a yelp, both young men bolted up and fled the kitchen, tumbling pell-mell out the back door and vaulting over the porch to the frozen ground.

The following summer, another friend of Kim's brother awoke early one morning to see a man standing at his bedroom window, staring dreamily out to sea. Wearing clothes of another era—possibly the 1920s—the specter appeared unaware of the living occupant of the room, as if his own visit of long ago had, in some strange abracadabra of time, transposed itself on the present weekend.

Before the Angells moved into what they always referred to as the "Big House," the residence resonated with the piano and violin duets, dramatic dialogue, tap of *pointe*-shoes, and dab of paint brushes of Miss Kathleen Hinni's School of Creative Arts. In those days—the 1940s and 1950s—the seven-and-a-half acres contained, in addition to the imposing main house, an assembly hall, various smaller buildings, and fifteen little cabins. The artistic summer camp catered to children aged from six to twenty and, in the thirteen years of its existence, grew from eighteen pupils and five staff members to eighty pupils and twenty staff members. An old brochure offered eight weeks of creative enrichment for the grand total of $450 (the equivalent of several thousand dollars today). During the 1920s and 1930s, the YMCA supervised Camp Winnecunnet on the site. That organization had, in turn, purchased the estate from Mr. Walter Soren in 1922.

West Chop's gilded age spanned from the 1890s to the late 1930s, when the sprawling seaside manor houses sprang up along the bluffs, and the peninsula served as the playground for the families of Boston Brahmin. A West Chopper's diary dated August 4, 1906, paints a picture of the quintessential privileged holiday: "Summer was forever in those days. We came in June and left in September. We were so busy that we didn't have time for everything. I had to exercise my horse before breakfast in order to get to tennis so we could go swimming so we could go sailing." And from another summer sojourner's journal: "Harry had a fine sail, [played] tennis, [took] a bath and [enjoyed] moonlight canoeing before a giddy evening at the Casino with the young ladies of the Chop."

If today the ghosts of the Big House are the wraiths of Boston gentry, happy campers, summer thespians, musicians, painters, and balletomanes, then it's easier to understand their winter petulance. Their rosiest memories are stirred by hot sunshine dappling the water, violets floating in cut-crystal punch bowls, and the calliope of the organ grinder, imported along with his monkey, for a party on a vast expanse of emerald green lawn.

The haunting of the Big House, although it occasionally administered some shocks to unsuspecting visitors, rarely presented itself as a problem to the family. "We basically felt protected by the spirits," says Kim today. "We got the feeling that so many people had been happy there and that they'd come back to enjoy some more good times."

Kim's parents recently sold the mansion, much to the younger Angell's deep regret. "I feel so sad my children will never experience those wonderful West Chop summers," Kim confides. But other long-term residents—the restless guardians of the Angell manor—may have found it unnecessary to leave, and conceivably, they'll go on making themselves quite at home, particularly in the off-season when the drafty halls are ceded back to them.

8

The Amorous Ghost

FEW YEARS AGO, when Kathy Appert bought the Victorian Inn on South Water Street, she never for a moment thought that the house built by Captain Lafayette Rowley in 1857 might be haunted.

Tall windows and white Corinthian columns face the narrow lane with a grace and purity typical of the grander homes erected in the second half of the nineteenth century. The mansard roof, added in the 1980s, altered a steeply pitched attic space into a highly serviceable third floor. Inside the inn, the window lace is homey and the antique furniture is handsome yet reassuringly lived in. A four-poster bed, cozy comforter, and a teddy bear adorn each bedroom; you feel you've entered an actual Victorian abode rather than the too-glossy reproduction from a decorator's sourcebook.

During Kathy's first night in the new property, empty except for herself and the previous owners, she slept soundly without a single interruption, but in the morning, before she descended the stairs, something startled her. Behind the paneled door of one of the rooms, the sound of a woman's laughter could be heard. It was an infectious laugh, rich and melodious, and Kathy was filled with an overwhelming desire to meet this person.

"I must be imagining things," she told the previous owners, a husband and wife, when she joined them in the breakfast room downstairs. Intrigued and confused, she described the laugh.

The couple traded a meaningful glance. They appeared to make up their minds about something. The woman turned to the new owner and announced, "We have a ghost. Or actually several ghosts."

Kathy was reluctant to accept this as a valid interpretation of the peal of laughter heard upstairs and, for two months, nothing unusual transpired at the inn. Then one day when Kathy and a young helper named Laura applied themselves to a furious spring cleaning, Kathy experienced her second brush with the supernatural.

While the new owner tackled the downstairs public rooms, Laura scrubbed, dusted, and vacuumed the bedrooms on the second and third stories. Every so often, when Kathy chanced to glance up the staircase, she caught glimpses of Laura in the white drawstring jacket she wore—

like a smock favored by a lab technician. As the girl scooted around corners, the white cotton billowed behind her. At last, at the end of a long workday, Kathy decided it was time to quit. Poised at the bottom of the ground-floor stairs, she called for Laura. No answer. Mounting the steps, she paused at the second-floor landing, again calling out her assistant's name. Directly overhead, she saw a figure flit around a corner, that same swish of white cotton fluttering behind it. "Laura!" she called again.

She felt a tap on her shoulder. Spinning around, she found Laura grinning at her. "Why were you shouting upstairs?" Laura asked. "I've been doing the laundry on the ground-floor for the past few hours!"

Kathy blanched and replied, "I think I just saw the ghost."

Over the next few seasons, her customers saw ghosts, too. On any given morning, a guest might wander into the breakfast room looking thoughtful and subdued. There, in the cheerful room with floral print tablecloths and vases of lobelia and baby's breath on each table, he or she would sheepishly ask the innkeeper, "Do you know you have a ghost?"

On a warm night in August, a Boston couple left the inn to carouse about town. They enjoyed a large meal followed by the basic Edgartown pub crawl in the tradition of the sailors who in the "Shiver me timbers" days swarmed the busy seaport. Past two o'clock in the morning, they collapsed into bed. Their lights were the last to blink off in the Victorian Inn that night.

An hour or so later, the man sputtered awake in what felt like the grip of an angina attack. Opening his eyes, he was amazed to find a man seated imperturbably on his chest. Wearing the black, high-collared frock coat of a proper Victorian gentleman, the apparition appeared to be tall, tanned, and clean-shaven, with a mane of silver hair brushed back from an angular, slightly sneering, face.

The tourist took one long incredulous look, then dived back into the oblivion of sleep in that psychological dodge of pulling the plug on reality. The next morning, the man awoke with the memory of the chest-squatter fresh in his mind. He decided he'd indulged in too much drink the evening before, and, while he'd never in his life hallucinated, he silently pledged to cut down on the eighty proof.

At his side, his wife stirred awake, a bewildered expression on her face. She told him, "I had the strangest dream! I thought I woke up and saw a man sitting on your chest!" She added that the oddest element about the dream was that it hadn't felt remotely dreamlike; she was convinced, at the time, that it was happening.

Not very long ago, a young woman from the New York publishing world checked into an airy room upstairs. The room has tall windows overlooking the harbor and a set of French doors opening onto a wide balcony. Past midnight, the woman awoke to see one of the balcony doors blow open and a tall, tanned man with a mane of silver hair stride into the room. Frozen in a helpless supine position, the woman watched him approach. When he reached her bed, he extended a long arm, and, with thumb and forefinger, tweaked her left nipple.

Her fear immobilized her as the figure with a roguish grin seemed to ask, "Am I not the sexiest ghost in all of New England?" He then glided back toward the balcony, exited cleanly, and closed the door behind him.

No sooner had the woman taken her first breath in a full minute when the adjacent balcony door burst open.

Standing outside, five men prepared to enter. Clad in layers of worn, old-fashioned garments, the men presented the hairy look of long-ago mariners, with shaggy beards, muttonchop side whiskers, and bristling mustaches. From the bed, the young woman watched aghast as they moved forward into the room. At last she found her voice and, bolting straight up from the pillows, shouted, "Go away!"

They vanished.

In addition to these alarming apparitions, the previous owners reported that during their reign, a certain prankish poltergeist infested the inn. During the night, furniture would be cast into the hall. One morning a bulky wicker chair was discovered tightly wedged into the small closet of an unoccupied room. It required the tugging and straining of two strong employees to wrench it loose. In another room, the cleaning staff regularly encountered a collection of old-fashioned hairpins scattered over the same section of carpet. Often the women inhabiting that room during the times when the clips appeared sported short coifs that would never require any sort of hairpin, much less the out-of-date type once used for securing long braids or chignons or straw boaters.

A couple of years ago, Kathy's daughter was engaged in tidying an upstairs chamber. When she approached the tousled sheets, she heard a man's voice growl, close at hand, "Get out!" But when she whirled around to see who was speaking, no one was there. On other occasions, several guests reported waking late at night to behold a gentleman in a dark suit seated in an armchair across the room, the visitor oblivious to their presence as he calmly smoked a pipe.

Shortly after the young woman in the publishing trade witnessed the five phantoms attempting to invade her room, Kathy decided something had to be done about her nonpaying customers. The least desirable development would be for people to stay away from the inn for fear of colliding with those things that as youngsters we are told categorically will *not* go bump in the night. In the company of several sympathetic friends, Kathy conducted a cleansing ritual. They burned banishing herbs such as burdock and lavender and, lighting an assortment of candles, exhorted the spirits to leave them in peace.

Kathy is convinced that since the ceremony, the more extreme disturbances have ceased, though she's had indications that ghosts still linger to play a trick or two, perhaps to keep a hand in. So who's behind the haunting of the elegant Victorian Inn? What cast of characters has emerged from the theater of history to meld with the present moment? And why?

Kathy's strongest hunch was that it had something to do with the original owner. Oddly enough, not a single descendant of Captain Lafayette Rowley of South Water Street remains on the island to provide an oral history of his or her ancestor. Past 1900, Captain Rowley's widow and their five offspring dispersed to the Boston area and Cape Cod. This in itself defies both tradition and demography, for the Vineyard has a way of bewitching its residents and, in any large family, two or three or more of the children or grandchildren inevitably stay on and put down roots. The decampment of the Rowley family raises an interesting conjecture: Is it possible that as early as the 1850s, the gracious house on South Water Street already hosted its complement of ghosts?

In Lafayette Rowley's action-packed career at sea, the opportunity was rife for attracting restless spirits and unwittingly carting them home with him, along with enameled pottery from China and bright baubles from the Antipodes.

Born in Greenport, Long Island, the son of a master mariner, Lafayette Rowley signed up for his first whaling voyage at the tender age of fifteen. Due to expectations that he would follow in his father's footsteps and as a result of his innate sailing acumen, the boy was drilled in navigational skills far beyond what was generally taught to a lowly cabin boy. Consequently, when the captain and first mate died of scurvy, the crew relied on the mere slip of a lad to guide them safely back to Greenport. His courage and skill were duly noted and it wasn't long before he was given the helm of his own ship. Over the course of his distinguished career, he served as master mariner of the *Orozimbo*, the *Junior*, the *Citizen*, and the *Neptune*.

One harrowing tale of the sea provides another backdrop for ghost-making in Captain Rowley's life. In 1856, Rowley's predecessor at the helm of the *Junior*, Captain Thomas Mellen, also of Martha's Vineyard, picked up a fresh crew of men in New Bedford for the whaling ship's long voyage to the South Seas. From the start, Mellen's veteran sailors shrank from the company of the newcomers. The recent recruits seemed sinister and unfriendly and, more alarming, they engaged in minor acts of rebellion such as refusing, when stationed high on the mast, to announce the sighting of whales.

One hundred and fifty-six days into the voyage, several miles off the coast of New Zealand, the New Bedford gang swilled spirits from coconut shells to give them courage, then flourished the pistols they'd concealed in their kit bags, and proceeded to murder the captain and first mate in their cabins. The date was December 25, 1856. When later the thugs weighted the captain down and pitched him overboard, their leader, Cyrus Plummer, cried out, "Go down to Hell and tell the Devil I sent you!"

This ill-fated ship, cleaned up and refitted, was transferred to Lafayette Rowley to captain in the same year that he built his future family's home. It's tempting to speculate that Captain Rowley, in taking charge of the *Junior*, stepped aboard a veritable floating hostelry of ghosts—possibly the murdered Mellen and his second-in-command or perhaps the malevolent mutineers or maybe even both sides of the Christmas slaughter. Certainly, here in the present day, the female guest who turned away from her room five ancient mariners saw something approaching a delegation from the hapless *Junior*.

By the early 1850s, Captain Rowley decided to make Martha's Vineyard, repository for master mariners everywhere, his home. In a socioeconomic move common for the times, he agreed to become affianced to either Rebecca or Sophronia Worth of Edgartown; no records remain to indicate which one. The Worths, as an old Vineyard family, with pre-Revolutionary soldiers, assorted sea captains, and military men in their family tree, (including General William J. Worth, hero of the Mexican War), probably outclassed the newcomer from Greenport. But a young whaling captain with a number of successful voyages under his belt and a fortune to lavish on his future wife, family, and home, would have appealed to the Edgartown gentry, and either Rebecca or Sophronia was to be counted among the lucky young ladies in town.

Then one day in church Lafayette Rowley set eyes on the third Worth daughter, Eliza Ann. No portraits or diaries remain, and no oral history survives to flesh out the tale. All that's left is a handful of terse entries in a ledger at the Edgartown Hall of Records: Eliza Ann Worth married

Lafayette Rowley on August 27, 1854. He was thirty, she twenty-four. On August 26, 1857, Captain Rowley paid five hundred dollars to Thomas Milton for a parcel of property including the southwesterly half of the dwelling and outbuildings already located on said lot. On the twenty-eighth, for an additional five hundred dollars, Rowley bought an adjacent parcel of land from Hannah Worth (the bride's widowed mother), Rebecca Worth, and Sophronia Worth (the bride's sisters), both classified in the ledger as "spinsters," one of whom was, to add insult to injury, the rejected fiancee.

Nearly a century and a half later, we can only read between the lines to resurrect an ancient heartache.

One final adventure awaited Captain Lafayette Rowley at sea. During his homeward-bound whaling excursion in 1864, while rounding the coast of the Carolinas, he successfully eluded the Confederate raider, the *Alabama*. He spent the remainder of his days in well-earned retirement in Edgartown.

The closing records read as follows: Lafayette Rowley died at home on August 4, 1900. Eliza Worth Rowley died in 1910 in Lowell, Massachusetts. She, like her children, cleared out of the house on South Water Street, never to return. Or did she? Or he? Or any of them?

9

One for the
(Other World) Road

NOTHING ABOUT the charming circa 1750 farmhouse on Atwood Circle suggested to Mrs. Helen Bowring that she and her husband, E. Bonner Bowring, had erred in purchasing it. In the spring of 1950 she left her apartment in Manhattan to spend some hectic but, she felt certain, satisfying weeks adapting the Edgartown home to her needs and those of Mr. Bowring who would join her for the summer.

The first day she cleaned, shopped, and, with a practiced eye, planned her interior decoration. The rambling, low-ceilinged, two-story home abounded with antique double-hung windows overlooking meadows and fields that had once accompanied the property.

That first evening, alone in the upstairs master bedroom, the absolute stillness of the countryside unsettled her, accustomed as she was to the constant clamor of Manhattan. The darkness also took some adjusting to, though a column of moonlight did shine through the windows, illuminating the hardwood floor and ornate oak door, which, like all the interior doors in the house, displayed an upper panel of wavy, antique, bull's-eye glass.

And then she heard it.

It seemed to be coming from the stairwell; the unmistakable sound of a heavy footfall. Whoever mounted the stairs stopped just short of Mrs. Bowring's door. Trembling beneath her covers, she stared at the bull's-eye glass but discerned no one through the semi-opaque view of the hallway. Still shaking, Mrs. Bowring burrowed down beneath the blankets and willed herself to sleep.

Hoping the episode would prove nothing more than a bad dream or some eccentricity of architecture, easily explained by anyone who understood the quirks of elderly houses, Mrs. Bowring retired to bed for the second night in her unfamiliar abode. She turned off the light and waited expectantly. Once again she heard footsteps ascending the stairs. By the third night she could only fall asleep with the tranquilizing aid of a snifter of brandy.

When Mr. Bowring arrived from the city, his energy that should have been expended moving furniture and digging rose gardens was redirected toward calming his wife. He reasoned that no ghost could possibly be stalking their staircase because ghosts, as any fool knew, did not, never had, and never would exist. Convinced his wife displayed a typically female predisposition to hysteria, Mr. Bowring switched off the light and wished her an irritable good night.

Suddenly he bolted up from the pillow as he too heard footsteps on the stairs. When the intruder reached the upper landing, Mr. Bowring threw off the covers and lunged for the door. Flinging it open, he roared, "Who the hell's in my house?"

No one presented himself.

Before many more days had elapsed, the Bowrings, now mutually persuaded their house was haunted, grew despondent at the thought of having to live indefinitely with their stair-climbing phantom. Somehow this violated their notion of the perfect country home.

Mr. Bowring began to make discreet inquiries in the village. Soon he learned the man to consult was a certain Edgartown personality named Manuel Swartz Roberts. A genial raconteur, termed by a writer at the *Vineyard Gazette* as a "boatbuilder, craftsman, and philosopher," Mr. Swartz Roberts's workshop down by the Chappaquiddick ferry wharf was a well-known hangout for locals of all ages and occupations. On stormy nights when passage across the harbor was barred, the stranded residents of Chappy (as Chappaquiddick Island is commonly known), schoolchildren included, would sit around the boatbuilder's cozy quarters, its weathered walls warmed by the blast of the steam boiler. Here every anecdote, every news event, and every scrap of gossip about the area would be trotted out and swapped as verbal barter. Thus, it was no wonder Mr. Swartz Roberts was famed for his wide knowledge of local history and island lore.

The Bowrings paid Mr. Swartz Roberts a call at his

workshop strewn with wood shavings and rusted relics from the sea. (When the boatbuilder died, by the way, he bequeathed the picturesque studio to local artists and it now stands as the well-loved Old Sculpin Gallery.) There, in the spring of 1950, Mr. Swartz Roberts listened to Mr. and Mrs. Bowring's story with narrowed, twinkling eyes. The expression on his sun-leathered face altered not in the slightest as he flatly told them, "That's old Allen Mayhew haunting your place. Used to be his farm. I'll tell you how to lay him back to rest."

Allen Mayhew, one of the many descendants of the 1660s first founding family of Governor Thomas Mayhew, had indeed farmed the acreage near the Edgartown harborfront. Born in 1843, the son of an Edgartown attorney, he had turned his back on opportunities for a professional life and had instead struggled to coax crops from ungenerous soil. He died shortly after World War I. In the 1920s, Eleanor and Clark Atwood bought the old farmstead along with the adjoining Modley place, modernized both of them, moved a hill that blocked their seaview, and filled in the swampy land on all sides. Strangely enough, over the years these two homes off Dunham Road attracted a reputation for being haunted. Today, Manuel Swartz Roberts's successor as the island Homer, a gentleman named Milton Jeffers, who himself was one of the Chappy schoolchildren often stranded in the boatbuilder's sociable workshop, maintains that the Modley house in particular, deserted for years, was a source of fascination and terror for youngsters in the area.

When Manuel Swartz Roberts related to the Bowrings everything he knew about Allen Mayhew's homestead, he delivered the remedy for dispatching the old farmer's spirit from their dwelling: "Every night before you retire, set out a bottle of Jack Daniel's whisky on the bottom step of your staircase, along with an empty shot glass. He won't actually partake of the liquor, but he'll appreciate the gesture. It's your way of saying he's welcome in your house. Don't forget, he still thinks it's *his* house. If you humor him in this way, he'll stop staking out his territory."

That evening the Bowrings followed the boatbuilder's instructions to the letter. To their immense surprise and relief, they heard no more footsteps mounting the stairs. They continued to follow this practice every night for many years. When every so often they neglected to set out the libation, the ghost revived his audible trek up the stairs. And he added a new feature to his ghostly trick-or-treats: One day Mrs. Bowring was aware of someone rambling across the floorboards of the den. Situated in the next room, she heard a familiar *phlumph* sound and the sigh of leather as a body settled into the large brown armchair facing the fireplace. Thinking her husband had returned early from his morning jaunt to the village, she entered the room framing the question, "What would you like for lunch, dear?"

She found an empty chair.

Over the years, the footsteps on the stairs and the slow easing into the armchair continued to disturb the household whenever the ceremonial drink was omitted from the Bowring's bedtime ritual. Then in 1983 Mr. Bowring died, and from that point on, the hauntings ceased.

As I sat with Mrs. Bowring in the den of her antique farmhouse (myself positioned, as I realized with mild apprehension, in the ghost's favorite armchair), I asked her if she believed her husband's spirit might have, on his way to the next world, made a last stop at the house to lure the problematic ghost away with him.

"That's possible," she replied with a thoughtful nod. "Old Allen Mayhew is gone, but in the last two years I've been visited by no less than five ghosts."

I shot up in the famously noisy chair. "Five? Are you kidding?" I asked incredulously.

She then told me that the first time she saw them she'd awakened from a deep sleep with a sense that something was amiss. Sitting up in bed, her eyes had been drawn to the bull's-eye window in the door. From down below in the living room, the light from a plant-growing bulb had cast a faint glow up the stairwell. Peering in through the thick wavy glass as if trying to pinpoint her location, the faces of five separate men had taken turns at the station, each one blending into the next like the slow dissolves of a film montage. "They had the hairy faces of old-time sailors," she said, "with long beards and muttonchop side whiskers."

On several other occasions, Mrs. Bowring has awakened in the night to glimpse the small band of ancient mariners. Although frightened by the tableaux, she nonetheless comforts herself with the conviction that the phantoms would be hard put, as they stand in relative light, to perceive her in the darkened bedroom.

So the lovely renovated farmhouse on Atwood Circle remains gently haunted, a fact driven home to me on that balmy day in June as I sat listening to Mrs. Bowring's story.

"Do you get the impression that Allen Mayhew is totally, irrevocably gone?" I asked.

Mrs. Bowring had no opportunity to answer, for just as I posed the question, the door between the den and the dining room—with no breath of air stirring outside—slowly swung from a wide-open position to a creaking close, shutting with a little snap as if an unseen hand made certain that nothing out of the ordinary could propel it open again.

10
The Ghostly Love Muse

THE SOUNDS AND SIGHTS OF THE OCEAN are beautiful and we regret going back to land-locked Minneapolis. We came here and learned more about ourselves as a couple, rediscovering what our love is and how strong it will always be. I know now I must have her with me forever."

This entry in the Oak House's Tiffany Room log is typical of the romantic musings of its many guests. The small diary with its cover of pink rosebuds on blue chintz is filled with passages of the bliss of loving couples. Another entry dated June 6, 1992, reads: "If you come to the

Oak House thinking you are in love, you may leave with more love than you ever dreamed possible. New love or old love rekindled. I hope future guests will leave as I did— with the passion of their dreams."

Of course, the setting and decor of the room must account for many of these amorous stirrings. Cradled on the third floor, the Tiffany Room's circle head of stained glass above the dormer window catches the first rays of sunrise, absorbs them into its own red and amber hues, then refracts them into the room in roving prism dots of dazzling light. The quaintly sloped ceiling, lace curtains, brass bed, and white carpet unite to form a bower in which even the most hardhearted might be tempted to fall in love: "Be they n'er so vile, this day will gentle their condition," as Shakespeare's Henry V so eloquently put it.

And, needless to say, vile people would never seek to come here. The guests are already predisposed toward a romantic vacation. No one reserves a room at a seaside bed and breakfast renowned for its charm and beauty without a certain sentimental agenda in mind. And yet, despite the fact that the other rooms at the Oak House are equally picturesque, judging from the entries in all the diaries and also from announcements made over breakfast downstairs, it is inarguably the Tiffany Room that inspires the lion's share of engagements, renewed vows, and R and R's transformed into honeymoons.

And it is the Tiffany Room that harbors the ghost.

A log entry for August 8, 1992, reads: "Looking out the middle window I saw a figure that looked like a ghost. Not a nasty one. The pose reminded me of the statue, 'The Thinker.'"

Another entry on July 28, 1993, reads: "She [the ghost] was older but not old, heavy-set, and moved with grace. As she stood by the white floor-lamp [sic], she looked back at me and smiled reassuringly. Taking the lamp in both hands, she rocked it back and forth as she stared out to sea. I have never believed in ghosts or psychic phenomena, but [I] could not rationalize away what happened. She was there and then she was gone."

Not all the disturbances involve actual sightings. Many guests have reported mysterious footsteps on the stairs, a voice in the room—sometimes a man's, sometimes a woman's—and just outside the window, the sound of wind chimes, even though none exist anywhere on the premises.

In 1872 Samuel Freeman Pratt (the Boston architect responsible for many of Newport's luxurious, albeit over-dressed mansions), renovated the cottage on the Oak Bluffs' boardwalk. The most dramatic element of Pratt's vision involved slicing the second floor from the first, then filling the architectural sandwich with a new second floor in order to preserve the fetching mansard roof line with its gables and vaguely Gothic dormer facing the sea. William Claflin, governor of Massachusetts from 1869 to 1872, bought the house and successive owners have respected and preserved the oak-paneled walls, leaded windows, and gingerbread flourishes. Today's inn still presides over the boardwalk like a bejeweled Victorian lady with a firm sense of her own entitlement to so spectacular a view.

In 1987 the Convery family of Edgartown pooled their resources to buy and manage the inn. Betsi Convery had recently earned a college degree in hotel administration. Her father, Leo, with his many years in real estate, handled the business aspects. His wife, Alison, a professional decorator, rolled up her sleeves to restore the house to its former glory. Betsi's sister Susan flew back from Brazil to cheer the effort on and to pitch in wherever needed.

The following spring the Oak House opened for business. One Saturday night at about ten o'clock, with most of the guests still out on the town, night manager Dan Harper sat alone in the kitchen. The empty house creaked all around him with the sounds that old buildings specialize in. Suddenly Dan heard someone call his name. Thinking his wife, Cara, had returned from her own evening sortie, he went to look for her. Cara was nowhere to be found. When sometime later she reappeared, she found her husband looking pale and slightly distraught.

About a week later, Betsi Convery sat alone in the kitchen at roughly the same time in the evening. From the next room she heard a distinct summons: "Betsi." She, too, wandered the house in search of the caller and found no one. "Ever since that night," she confides today, "I've hesitated to spend a minute alone at the inn."

Betsi's husband, Mark Luce, has never seen or heard the ghost. "It doesn't show itself to many people," reports Betsi. "Apart from those two episodes in the kitchen, mainly people in the Tiffany Room have had experiences. And once in another room on the second floor—the room where we've hung an antique christening gown—a woman, after settling down for a nap, heard a child's footsteps cross the floor. She felt a cold little hand slip into hers but when she turned to look, no one was there."

Contacted by telephone, a guest from last summer had this story to tell about his stay in the Tiffany Room: "My wife was fast asleep, but I woke up in the middle of the night to see this woman hovering over me in a helpful kind of way—like a mom about to feel your forehead. I was so groggy, I thought someone human had walked into the room, and then I realized I was staring right through her! She was transparent! But the weirdest part is that she started to say, 'I must tell you something . . . ' and then she disappeared! When I told my wife about it the next morning, it just killed her not to know what the ghost's message was."

When asked to describe the apparition, the man responded, "She was about fifty years old, I think, with gray hair done up in a fancy style, and she wore an old-fashioned white nightgown—sort of lacy—do you know what I mean?"

I put one more question to the guest: Did he and his wife enjoy a romantic holiday? "Oh yeah!" he replied with a private chuckle. "I convinced her to keep me around for another couple of years." Then in a softer tone, he confided, "We decided that weekend to renew our vows. Maybe back on the Vineyard next summer."

So who are these spirits who lurk on the third floor of the Oak House to inspire lovers to love still more, with all the poetry buried deep in their souls? At the start of each new season, this Victorian valentine of a hotel room waits for new subjects, ready to enfold them in the embrace of its soft-as-velvet heart.

11

A Way Station for Wandering Spirits

CANDACE DUARTE* is the sort of ethereal person to whom ghosts and strange psychic phenomena have always attached themselves. For this reason she is the perfect occupant for Hadley House,* a beautifully restored seventeenth-century manor up-island, a residence which has always attracted stuff and matter from other dimensions.

Once, when Candace was a little girl growing up on a country estate in Connecticut, she found herself behind her mother's garden on a wildflower-flecked plain she had never seen before. There she met a kindly, wizened man who spoke to her at length about her family and who seemed to intuit her innermost thoughts. When Candace returned home, she related her adventure. Her mother's face turned white with consternation. "Take me there now!" she demanded. But when the little girl led the way through the garden and up the rise to the plain, she found nothing except the old familiar stretch of lawn and orchard. What dimension had she entered for that spellbinding hour?

Another startling event occurred years later one rainy afternoon as she sped down a highway in her car. All of a sudden a semitransparent figure of a woman appeared splayed across her hood, her face pressed to the windshield. "Pull over!" shouted the figure. Stunned, Candace could only stare through the glass. "Pull over!" repeated the apparition, growing more agitated by the second, "Now!" When Candace, still too shocked to react, continued to numbly drive the car, the figure projected images to Candace's mind that appeared with the clarity of a video: She saw her own car rolling over and over a highway embankment until it crashed at the bottom of a hill. At last Candace acted, swerving to the shoulder of the road. As she braked to a halt, two events occurred simultaneously: the woman disappeared and the rear right wheel popped free of its axle, falling off the car.

Finally, before she moved to Hadley House on Martha's Vineyard, Candace found herself in the midst of a particularly sinister occult ambience in an old hunting lodge in Vermont. Having settled in with a small band of friends, she and her roommates all reported the same chilling phenomenon: Every time any one of them bent over for

*Names changed to protect confidentiality

any reason—to tie a shoe or to pick something up—each experienced the daunting sensation that someone stood over him or her with an upraised ax. Moreover, strange sounds—chopping noises, and the snap of branches—for which they could find no visible source, dogged their footsteps when they walked in the hundreds of acres of woods.

At last the frightened tenants sought information from the town records. They learned that, some years before, a lumberjack who had lived in the hunting lodge had gone berserk and had taken an ax to his wife and child, killing them. Outraged, the townspeople had tracked him down and strung him up in the woods.

Candace and her friends knew that something had to give: either they or the troubled spirit would need to depart. They consulted a psychic in the city and were told that their ghost was trapped in his own hell of guilt and depravity. What he needed was to be humored out of his anguish—only levity would lighten him enough to move him along to the next world. For the next few weeks, Candace and her friends spent evenings in the hunting lodge swilling wine, telling jokes, and acting goofy. "We made him laugh," reported Candace, "and then one day his presence vanished from the lodge. I think he was fortunate to find people who were willing to work with him. Without the effort we put into liberating him, he'd still be there scaring the daylights out of people."

When Candace and her husband moved into Hadley House, Candace with her lifelong sensitivities to other realities, was immediately and yet comfortably aware of spirits in the rambling house with its low-beamed ceilings and sloping floors. The original wing was built in 1670 by Thomas Church who subsequently sold it to Thomas Merry, an Indian fighter from the mainland. (Although

Merry made a life for himself on the Vineyard—wedding a girl from Braintree and siring six children—he was nonetheless bored with no hostile Indians to slaughter. But possibly his ennui fed into his longevity for he died at the age of one hundred and five, while plowing a field across the road.) In time, new generations added other wings to the house, all of them designed with picturesque nonconformity. Even the ghosts seem to have blended right in with the home's charm and whimsy.

"Sometimes I'd come upon a very quiet old lady sitting in the red leather wing chair in the front parlor," reported Candace. "There was another spirit that we only heard. Late at night she would sing opera along with some sort of musical accompaniment. It turns out that in the last century a singer married into the Look family and she lived in a little cottage on the property. She had a nice, rich soprano voice but sometimes she would wake us up in the middle of the night, and my husband would grump at me, 'Tell her to shut up!'"

Candace had her favorite spirit: a young man, extremely handsome and zestful, clad in what she described as a Mardi Gras costume: "He wore a black mask over his eyes, a tight black satin vest, and a shirt with a white ruffle at the neckline." She added, "He used to frighten my guests because he would stand on the landing of the circular staircase and they wouldn't see him until they'd almost reached the top. But sometimes he'd appear to me when I was feeling depressed about something and, I don't know what it was about him, he always cheered me up."

It was for the sake of her many houseguests that Candace finally toyed with the idea of exorcising the spirits. As she recalled, "There was so much coming and going of supernatural material, I wondered if the house was centered on some kind of dividing line between different worlds." Candace and I discussed this one day and I told her what I'd learned in my own research: that many scholars of the paranormal believe that certain locations on the planet constellate the sorts of energies that involve ingress and egress from one plane to the next. Chicago, for instance, is reputed to have more blowing through it than its famous winds.

During a subsequent meeting with Candace, however, she offered a new theory: She'd learned that the house perched over a shallow aquifer. "There's a body of water running underneath the land," she said, "and I think it makes for a certain fluidity of a psychic nature above ground."

Whatever the reason, some of Candace's easily spooked friends were finding time spent at Hadley House tough going. One night a man and his two young daughters bedded down in the guest quarters across the circular drive. Past midnight the girls, who slept on a pull-out sofa near the front window, were awakened by a knock on the door. Their father sputtered awake and stumbled into the front room to see who'd summoned them at such an ungodly hour. He opened the door to see nothing more than the breeze ruffling the dark leaves, but to his horror and that of his daughters, all three of them distinctly heard the loud crunching sounds of footsteps across the gravel, retreating back to the main house. From upstairs in the main house, Candace heard the kitchen door open and close and then she listened to the tread of someone mounting the circular staircase, but she thought nothing of it. As has been mentioned before, the lady of the house had never been particularly troubled by the restless comings and goings of spirits. It was only in the morning when she learned of her guests' dismay that she forced herself to think about the anxiety level of others.

Another friend spoke of the time she'd wandered late at night from the kitchen to the pantry. As she neared the rear staircase, a wreath of dried flowers on the wall suddenly burst into flames. "I think I jumped up to the second floor without the benefit of stairs! That's how scared I was," she recounted later.

Candace gathered with a few friends to conduct a cleansing ceremony which consisted of asking God's help to permit the disoriented souls to find a more appropriate channel to work out their spiritual quest. Since the time of the ceremony, Hadley House has been pestered by nothing more than a troublesome early rising rooster.

From the tales I've collected, I've learned that spirits are amazingly amenable to orders to clear out. With the exception of Banquo's ghost who ignored Macbeth's command to "Avaunt and quit my sight," the chimeras from the Other Side, while they may frequently impinge on our privacy, respect our none-too-tactful hints to disperse when the time is appropriate. Perhaps in the natural order of things, the living are entitled to some kind of sovereignty here in our world of concrete and clay. The spirits, with their evident ability to shimmer through walls, to float, even to fly, or to light up like a beacon or vaporize into thin air—these transcendently mobile beings, some of them uncannily like angels—willingly cede to us our all-too-literal domain.

At Hadley House today, every so often something passes through, but Candace makes sure it keeps on going. She confided, "A couple of months ago, my husband and a friend and I were preparing dinner in the kitchen when we felt this freezing corridor of air move through the room. Our friend rapidly invoked a prayer over and over again, and we could all feel the entity waft through us, through the walls, and out of the house."

This last caller sounds like a fairly unwelcome and unwholesome guest, but, on the other hand, I think that for Candace, the nooks and crannies of Hadley House are slightly diminished without the playful appearances of the quiet old lady by the fire, the opera diva, and the Mardi Gras youth at the top of the stairs.

12

Windy Gates

IT'S AN ETERNAL TRUTH that if you surround yourself
with one hundred acres of sea-misty countryside,
you can comport yourself however you please and no
one need ever know about it. Accordingly, the lurid
history of the mysterious Lucy Sanford, who built Windy
Gates, may have been either imagined or wildly exagger-
ated by locals unused to the disportings of the rich and
decadent. But here are the facts—or distortions—as
chronicled in Vineyard writings over the last century.

Late in the 1890s, a still-beautiful, forty-something
widow named Lucy Sanford bought one thousand feet of

Chilmark beachfront and one hundred acres of cliffs and fields rising high above it. Her decision to acquire the land was an act of panicky escape. Having built a sumptuous castle called Fair Ladies in the Adirondacks, she and her summer neighbors had been plunged into indescribable terror when a series of murders by an unknown madman beset the resort. Lucy Sanford abandoned the castle forever. (As an intriguing footnote, it lay in ruins for decades.)

So Lucy found refuge on Martha's Vineyard. For the island's yeomanry in the late nineteenth century—fishermen, farmers, and carpenters—spending on the scale of Lucy Sanford's both dazzled them and outraged their sense of financial prudence. Yet everyone benefited from the construction of the mansion, carriage house, and stables at Windy Gates. Once or twice a week, Captain Zeb Tilton's schooner would unload materials at Menemsha Creek, where horse-drawn wagons would line up to convey lock, stock, and barrel to the Sanford property. Untold numbers of carpenters labored at the building site, along with masons, glaziers, furniture makers, and landscapers. The boon of work and income appeared limitless. Ever whimsical in her desires, Lucy would change her mind about a fountain or a staircase or a half-finished wing, demanding it be torn down and replaced with something altogether different. Many years elapsed before the last contractor and laborer walked away from the site.

Many of Lucy's design concepts proved utterly eccentric, such as her insistence on electrically lighting the tiled pigsties, this in an age when most Americans still lived by the glow of tallow or kerosene. The talk of the island for many years focused on the gold-plated bathroom fixtures upstairs in the main house. Before long the plate had changed to solid gold until the bathroom fairly shimmered in Vineyarders' imaginations as a vast gilded expanse, every last inch of which, from tiles to window sashes, had been fondled by King Midas himself. Those privileged few who had actually beheld the bathroom were invariably disappointed that all was not made of gold as the legend would have it and that, in fact, only the faucets were gold-plated, as originally stated.

In addition to this shortcoming, Lucy had never acquired a bathtub. She had once heard of an acquaintance who had drowned in a bath and the accident left her with a phobic abhorrence of anything containing more than an inch or two of water; thus she allowed only a low sitz bath to be installed in the "golden" bathroom.

Reading between the lines of Lucy's history, it's easy to see she must have suffered from some sort of nervous condition, if not utter hysteria. We can only wonder then how she responded to the bizarre *ménage à trois* that developed when her divorced daughter, Mary Kobbe, together with a mysterious young man named Jack Seals, arrived to live with her. The privacy afforded by one hundred wild acres kept the trio's lifestyle shielded from prying eyes, but island gossip has never been hampered by high walls and dense shrubbery. The word around the local taverns and kitchen tables was that mother, daughter, and imported boyfriend appeared uncommonly close, if not inseparable.

During her years on the windy moors of Chilmark, Lucy kept an elaborate carved box of pharmaceuticals on her dressing table. The high-strung widow displayed an expert knowledge of the cures and prescriptive doses of the dozens of stoppered bottles of distilled flowers and herbs which she kept lined up in little rows. Some of the vials contained heavy-duty barbiturates such as opium and laudanum, both perfectly legal over-the-counter patent medicines of the era. Soon neighbors learned of Lucy's ability as an unlicensed pharmacist, and patients with earaches or gout or indigestion arrived at her kitchen door for a cure drawn from one of her little glass flagons.

Shortly after the construction of the mansion was complete, Mary Kobbe traveled to Europe, where she met and married an Italian duke. She returned with him to Chilmark, where Jack Seals continued to live in grand style with Lucy. To resort once more to gossip—the only kind of oral history existing on the subject—the duke tyrannized his wife with perverse erotic wiles as well as dreams of grandeur. Spending at Windy Gates doubled, even tripled, as the former New York socialites were forced to entertain off-island visitors with lavish summer feasts and entertainments. The duke also induced his mother-in-law to stash all her remaining capital in South American railroads and bonds. The bonds crashed, and Lucy faced bankruptcy.

The time was optimum for the devious duke to, as the English say, "do a bolt." He deserted Mary, or so the story goes. At the time, certain islanders muttered that no one had actually witnessed his departure from the Vineyard, though none disputed the fact that he'd certainly disappeared. Soon thereafter Mary died of unknown causes. Then Jack Seals died. And Lucy Sanford's box of pharmaceuticals vanished forever.

Further reading between the lines might hint at some gruesome conclusions, but we must stick to the facts, bizarre enough in themselves: Lucy kept the ashes of both Mary and Jack in urns, and these two receptacles never left her side. When she traveled, the remains traveled with her, one vessel in each arm, and when her ruinous fortunes drove her from her elaborate home to a modest rooming house in Edgartown, the urns accompanied her into exile.

To this day, the hundred-acre oceanfront property remains intact. The mansion and picturesque carriage house appear much the same as they ever did, though the grounds have suffered from years of neglect. In the off-season, the estate has always attracted the lone hiker or romantic duo eager for a secluded place to share a bottle of wine, a loaf of bread, and whatever. It is during these impromptu excursions that the ghost has been sighted.

A couple of years ago in late October, a bird watcher from West Tisbury tromped across the open field near the carriage house. Boards covered most of the windows, and a typical look of seasonal abandonment hung over the place. Curious about the aged dwelling, he drew closer to peer inside. When his nose nearly touched the strip of antique glass beside the door, the figure of a man materialized only inches away on the other side of the window. The bird watcher gave out a holler of surprise, spun around, and fled across the field. For months he thought he'd encountered either a trespasser or a winter tenant—either way, a flesh-and-blood human being. But when in the spring he met up with the caretaker of Windy Gates at a bar in Oak Bluffs and mentioned the encounter, the latter shrugged and replied, "You saw the ghost."

Another time in warmer weather, a young man and woman spread picnic materials high on the bluffs of Windy Gates. With the sea shimmering before them and sunlight on their faces, they settled down on their blanket. Abruptly the woman gasped. Her companion snapped his head around in the direction in which she stared. Less than fifty yards away, a man stood amidst the wildflowers and stared back at them.

"He looked like someone out of 'Masterpiece Theatre,'" the woman reported later. "You know, with a long black jacket and a sort of brocaded vest."

At first the couple thought some up-island eccentric, of which there are many, was enjoying a daily constitutional clad in a costume purloined from his attic. But after scrambling to a sitting position, the couple turned to look again and saw that the man had disappeared. "There's no way he could have bundled out of there so fast," declared the woman. "It would have taken anyone several minutes to reach the far line of trees."

Other talk of ghost sightings at Windy Gates has often revolved around this figure of a man in Edwardian garb. Could it be the Italian duke? Jack Seals? Some long-ago visitor to Windy Gates who, after death, decided he'd like nothing better than to return to the site of a splendid Vineyard vacation? By most accounts, the ghost has filled his beholders with a sense of foreboding. A Gay Head landscaper who, like the bird watcher, had glimpsed the apparition in the carriage house, reported, "He [the ghost] had 'No Trespassing' written all over him!"

It's hard not to associate this image with the diabolical duke who exploited Mary and bilked poor Lucy out of her fortune. But had Lucy exacted the ultimate revenge by poisoning him and burying him on her extensive property? And does his ghost sometimes walk the grounds to rake up further mischief?

Others insist that the overall atmosphere of Windy Gates is hospitable and cheerful, and that everyone who has lived there, even if only for a month during the summer, has come away feeling renewed and refreshed. The reason for this could be another apparition spotted over the years, this one in the vicinity of the tennis courts or the little pond. A lady in white has materialized there, either traipsing through the woods or floating over the fields, her feet raised several inches from the ground.

Maybe the abiding spirit is Lucy Sanford herself, who, in spite of her obvious mental imbalance, was the first to love and nurture the property. It is she, perhaps, who spreads invisible arms over the mansion, the moors, and the glistening, unspoiled beach. And if the duke seeks to harm anyone, he'll have to reckon with Lucy. If the Chilmark lady millionaire had the last word in life, she might indeed continue to wield the last word in death.

13

Campground Gothic

SOME PEOPLE ARE SPOOKED by the Campground; most adore it. Those who find it mildly alarming tend to visit in the off-season when vacant rockers sit on empty porches and the array of jigsaw scrollwork and steepled windows might remind them of the fevered imagination of Stephen King, should he decide to center one of his novels in a demonic community of bizarre doll houses.

For those who love it, however, particularly in the summer when doors and windows stand open to fragrant breezes and neighbors can be found reading the newspaper on their porches and gardens are overflowing with lush blossoms, the Campground reigns as an absolute fairyland whose compressed infinity of wonders never ceases to amaze. In the labyrinth of parks and miniature Victorian manor houses, you can wander down a familiar lane and continue to spot elements never noticed before; an unexpected mansard roof, a carved wooden cat peeking from a gable, mint green trim and mauve shingles, or a riot of orange day lilies against a backdrop of pink astilbe.

What not everybody realizes, even fifth-generation Oak Bluffers, is that there wouldn't be an Oak Bluffs, or an Oak Bluffs as we know it, were it not for the Campground. Situated in a grove of ancient oaks beside the harbor, the community was established in 1835 as a religious retreat for Methodists; its primitive wood-planked preacher's stand and assortment of white canvas tents beckoning the faithful from all over New England. Each August the flock increased and before long the tents were converted into little houses, each one ornamented with newfangled gingerbread detailing supplied by Vineyard carpenters.

The beauty of the ceremonies, the enchanting cottages, and the heavily-wooded grounds illuminated by the glow of whale oil lanterns, drew large crowds of spectators. Hotels sprang up to billet these crowds and soon a group of canny developers decided to expand the architectural flavor of the Campground into secular developments. The homes of Oak Bluffs, though many of them have since been stripped of their towers, finials, and fretwork, were all enlarged Campground models set on wider plots of land. The town streets, like those of the Campground, meander in romantic, unpredictable patterns, each one encircling or ending in a half-forgotten park.

Susan Hidler spent every summer of her idyllic childhood at the Campground, and therefore she was especially pleased when in her early teens her parents bought one of the Victorian valentines. Though much of the raw charm of the dwelling remained, the cottage had fallen into disrepair when its previous owner, Mrs. Taylor, in the infirmity of old age, had neglected it. "We inherited all her frumpy furniture," confides Susan today, "and everything was dusty and rickety and badly in need of paint. For instance, the beautiful leaded windows were rimmed with clay to insulate them."

Mrs. Taylor moved to a nursing home in Florida and the Hidler family took up residence in the Campground cottage. Their first few summers passed without incident. Mrs. Hidler engaged in fix-up projects around the house while her two teen-aged daughters enjoyed their own activities around the Campground and up and down the block-long carnival known as Circuit Avenue. Then, back on the mainland on a winter day in the early 1970s, the Hidlers learned that Mrs. Taylor had died in Florida. The news struck them in a vague, abstract sort of way; they had met her only once or twice and she had made little impression on them.

The following summer, Susan, then eighteen and a freshman in college, in the company of a girlfriend, traveled to the island to open the cottage for the season. She said, "That first night at the house, we slept in the rear bedroom, at the back of which there's a door leading to the attic. There was a twin bed against each wall. In the middle of the night, in this pitch dark chamber, I heard what I thought was my friend walk between the two beds, open the attic door, and mount the stairs. So I said through the darkness, 'What are you doing? Where are you going?' and a quavery voice answered me from the other bed, 'What do you mean? What are you doing? Where are you going?' "

From that night forward the Hidler family knew that a ghost in a none-too-subtle way had taken up residence in their cottage. All summer long, Susan was awakened at night to find her bed shaking violently, first back and forth, then side to side. She would bolt up in bed shouting, "Stop it!" and the jostling would cease. Her sister, situated in the front bedroom overlooking the street, woke up one night as she felt the mattress cave in on one side of her bed. The covers had also been adjusted, as if someone had climbed into bed with her. Terrified, the girl ran from the room and refused to sleep there ever again.

At night the family and their visitors would lounge downstairs while unidentified footsteps tread the floorboards overhead or descended the stairs. At first the Hidlers found this disturbing, but after a while they accepted their ghost (whom they referred to as "Mrs. Taylor"), much as they might have resigned themselves to a noisy pipe or the nightly six o'clock carillon from the Campground bell tower.

From time to time, however, "Mrs. Taylor" made someone's flesh crawl. One night a male friend of Susan's sister sauntered up the walk and spotted a female figure in the upstairs front bedroom window. Assuming it was Susan's sister, he was surprised when a moment later she greeted him at the door. "I just saw you upstairs!" he cried. "No one's upstairs," she replied. They canvassed the group in the living room to learn that no one had ventured to the second floor in well over an hour.

Another night Susan and her boyfriend found themselves alone in the cottage. Just as they settled in for some snuggling on the sofa, the young man heard someone whisper something intently, though inaudibly, in his ear. He was suddenly overwhelmed with a sense of impending danger. "We've got to get out of here!" he exclaimed, dragging Susan from her own house.

By the following summer, "Mrs. Taylor" had apparently passed on to the next level. The cottage, in its absence of psychical substance, gave the Hidlers a final shudder, for the contrast between the home in its haunted state and in its quiet one reinforced just how disruptive the former had been.

The Campground, with its century-and-a-half of family histories, does continue to harbor ancestral spirits and wraiths of the night. In a cottage facing Sunset Lake, a musical ghost plays the piano in the front parlor. Other ghosts rap walls and misplace objects. In still another cottage, a family found itself thoroughly inconvenienced one summer by an old male ghost who monopolized the bathroom late at night.

So what vibration is it that visitors sense when they come upon the deserted verandas of the Campground on a cold autumn afternoon? Is it the wind scattering dead leaves that conveys a sense of unearthly desolation, or is it simply one's imagination that one of the empty rocking chairs has stirred into motion?

14

The Cat at the Funeral

S HE CAME TO MARTHA'S VINEYARD to heal a broken heart. Embroiled in a bitter divorce from her husband in Connecticut, Hooker Ackerman sought to get away from it all. She purchased a rustic house set on a rocky four-and-a-half-acre knoll in woodsy Oakdale, just inland from State Beach. With her two teenaged sons, her German shepherd, Shadow, and a deepening relationship with her good friend, John Farrar, who rented the guest house on her property, she was beginning to feel very nearly normal again; at anchor in a snug port.

Immediately following her fatal accident, the *Vineyard Gazette* described her as "a great beauty. Her grace of carriage, the classic features of her face, the charm of her manner, and her unusual height of more than six feet called to mind George du Maurier's now legendary figure, Trilby."

But we're getting ahead of the story. One rainy night in April 1965, Hooker drove into Vineyard Haven to pick up her young sons from the single theater open during the winter. They were nowhere to be found. Distraught, she returned home, wondering what to do. Should she call John? The police? Back at the house, the boys telephoned with a typical teen-aged, cockeyed story of how a friend had sidetracked them from the movie. They were now waiting at the theater to be collected. Relieved, but still jittery from the scare, she whistled for Shadow and they both jumped into the car for the drive back to Vineyard Haven.

It's possible the aborted crisis churned up fresh worries in Hooker's mind. As she sped along the slippery road, she might have also pondered anew how her sons were faring with the divorce and the move, particularly her thirteen-year-old, Hamilton, Jr., who had slipped into a protracted adolescent depression. (Sixteen years later he would die in a motorcycle accident; some conjectured it might have been a suicide.) Possibly distracted by her thoughts, Hooker may have paid scant attention to the tricky intersection of the Edgartown/Vineyard Haven and County Roads. Later the police speculated that her foot lunged for the brake but hit the accelerator instead. She smashed into a tree, flattening the car like an accordion. She and her German shepherd died instantly.

In an eerie presentiment of her son's death sixteen years later, talk of suicide floated about the Vineyard, but Hooker's friend John Farrar angrily resented it. Anguished

by her death, he knew better than anyone that Hooker had
begun to find peace and a sense of purpose here; she would
never take her own life, never. His most abiding regret was
that he'd had no chance to say goodbye to her. One day
they'd laughed and chatted happily together; the next a delegation of friends had appeared on his doorstep to tell him
she was gone.

A strange event occurred at Hooker's funeral. At the
onset of the graveside service, a black-and-white cat slinked
across the frosty mounds of the cemetery and delicately
approached the fresh black trench in the snow. Throughout the sermon and the singing of psalms, the creature
stood perfectly still, a single paw upraised, as it stared at
the shiny coffin poised over the pit. John Farrar was filled
with an uncanny sense that Hooker, who'd loved animals
and had herself possessed a feline grace, had returned in this
guise to attend her own funeral. The minister intoned a
prayer, and all bowed their heads, eyes closed. As a collec-
tive "Amen" filled the air, John raised his gaze. The cat
had vanished.

John's involvement with Hooker Ackerman's life was
fated to continue. Because he'd lent her the money for the
second mortgage on her house, it was to him that the property fell in what the law terms "involuntary alienation."
(The deceased woman's sons went to live with their father
in Connecticut.) John moved into the house and began a
long-term program of renovations. A personal renovation
also took place in his life. In the half-year since Hooker
had died, he had met a young woman, and, following a hot-
house courtship of a three-month duration, had married
her. They took up residence together in Hooker Ackerman's former house.

Shortly thereafter they heard noises in the attic—a

creaking tread, the faint sound of furniture being moved. John and his wife stared at one another with questioning eyes, but they shrugged it off; perhaps the timber in the frame was contracting, settling, whatever.

One day while John was in town, occupied with his work as an electrician and contractor, his wife arrived home with a new acquisition: a German shepherd puppy. As the puppy romped in the kitchen, the sounds in the attic intensified. The young woman tried to ignore them but before long she heard the unmistakable clomp of heavy-booted feet. The next thing she knew, a strong rumbling erupted, so profound it shook the ceiling and dimmed the lights. Terrified, she grabbed John's shotgun and aimed it at the trapdoor whose pull-down stairs vibrated from the unholy commotion.

At that precise moment, John returned home from work. His wife heard the kitchen door bang open and she spun around with the gun. From John's point of view, all he knew was that his bride was on the verge of blowing his head off. Stunned thoughts ran through his mind, along the lines of: Who is this woman? Is she psychotic? Did she plan all along to marry me and then pump me full of lead?

"What are you doing?" he shouted, grabbing blindly for the gun. She relinquished it and he broke it open, shaking out the shells.

Suddenly the rumbling exploded again and the trapdoor sprang open, the pull-down steps plunging halfway toward the floor. John and his wife stared in shock. Then John, wrenching free of his paralysis, rapidly reloaded the shotgun and pointed it through the open trapdoor. Immediately the steps lifted back up and the hatch closed with a *whomp*!

In a rage, John yanked at the rope that released the

pull-down steps. They clattered down into the kitchen and, weapon in hand, he charged up into the attic.

He found no one in the dingy recesses above. "I even got down on my hands and knees," he later reported, "dragging the shotgun along with me to look in every last nook and cranny up there. Nothing. I found nothing! But the one really upsetting feature was that a heavy trunk full of old nets and decoys had been hauled from one end of the attic to the other. Neither my wife nor I could understand how that happened."

Over the next few days the attic noises abated, but a strange new situation developed. It had been nine months since Hooker's death when a black-and-white cat (looking identical to the one John had observed at Hooker's funeral), showed up outside their house. Both John and his wife tried to ignore the visitor, but it refused to go unheeded. Any time of the day or night, John might look up to catch sight of it peering intently at him through a window. When at times John stepped outside to befriend the animal, it bolted for the surrounding woods.

One cold, still night John was alone in the house. As he sat reading in a reclining chair in the den, he was suddenly overwhelmed by the sense of a strong presence in the room with him. The hairs on the back of his neck stood up—a physical reaction he'd never experienced before. The feeling of visitation grew more intense until he felt as though he were being enfolded, embraced, touched by whatever invisible entity hovered over him. All at once he jerked up from the chair and reeled around. Directly outside the sliding glass door, illuminated by moonlight, the black-and-white cat stared at him. It opened its mouth in a long, drawn-out, silent yowl. Shocked, John fell back in the chair. When he looked again, the cat was gone.

He raced outside to check the pawprints in the snow. To his amazement, he saw the creature had circled the house time and again—perhaps as many as fifteen circuits, its tracks forming a necklace of patterns in its relentless circumnavigation of the house. But the most astonishing aspect of the cat's path was that not a single set of tracks could be seen going to or coming from the woods. The prints around the house appeared almost as if they'd been stamped by a circlet of paw designs floating down from the sky.

John felt certain the cat's appearance was Hooker's way of saying goodbye to him. "Not a single spooky incident ever disrupted the home again," he said. "I'm convinced Hooker appeared as a cat to view her own funeral, then again to check out the house. All that attic stuff was triggered by my getting married. She didn't like that. And, when my wife brought home the puppy, well, that was just too much for her, reminding her of Shadow, who died in the crash. But that last night when the cat circled the house and gave a silent yowl outside the window, that told me she was ready to let go."

15

Which Mrs. Hillman?

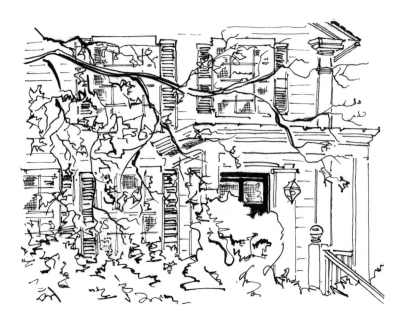

FATE SEEMED TO PLAY AN EERIE PART in luring Margaret Steele to buy the house on the corner of Cottage and Fuller Streets in Edgartown. A young mother with four little children and a year-round residence on the Connecticut shore, the last thing she needed was a large vacation house on Martha's Vineyard. Certainly her husband was dead set against the added responsibility. And yet Margaret had spent the summers of her childhood on the island and she felt compelled to invest in property there.

Her first day of house hunting floundered under a

misunderstanding. Margaret's parents had recently died, and, when a real estate agent asked her what she was looking for, she replied with morbid humor, "Something near a graveyard." The agent took her seriously and spent the day showing her houses abutting all the island's cemeteries. When Margaret realized the mistake, she set the agent straight but, all the same, none of the homes they viewed together excited the young woman's interest. And then they chanced to drive past the leafy intersection of Cottage and Fuller.

The Hillman house was very nearly ramshackle, with overgrown shrubs and ivy, peeling paint, and a nasty chainlink fence surrounding a yard of dead grass. And yet something about it plucked at Margaret's heartstrings. "That's the one!" she cried exultantly.

The agent was perplexed. "But it's not for sale," she said. On further consideration, however, she recalled that the house had been randomly—almost skittishly—placed on the market from time to time, but that the eccentric old lady who owned it had always withdrawn the property before anyone could become serious about it. Margaret felt strangely, almost obsessively determined and said, "Call her up. Make an appointment for me to inspect the house with a contractor."

To the agent's surprise, old Mrs. Hillman agreed to the plan. Apparently she'd known of Margaret all through the latter's childhood and early adulthood and had unilaterally approved of her. Margaret appeared on the premises with construction expert John Farrar (who has already made his appearance in "The Return of Desire" and "The Cat at the Funeral" stories). John combed the house with a discerning eye. While the contractor explored, the old lady in her stumbling gait crossed the dining-room floor to greet Margaret. Enfolding the young woman in a bone-crushing embrace, Mrs. Hillman chortled, "There'll be good times here again."

At the end of John's inspection, he announced that almost everything needed replacement or fortification, from the furnace to the plumbing to the wiring system. Margaret added up the cost of the major repairs together with the price of all necessary renovations to the interior spaces, façades, and grounds. She then deducted the sum from Mrs. Hillman's asking price.

On the same day that Margaret presented her offer, to be communicated via the real estate agent, old Mrs. Hillman died.

To this day, Margaret carries the uneasy sense that her reduced sales figure caused Mrs. Hillman's fatal heart attack. The two events seemed so extraordinarily synchronous: Only a few hours after Margaret called the agent, the agent telephoned back with news of the homeowner's passing. Margaret construed this as a sign that the issue was as dead as Mrs. Hillman, and she returned to Connecticut expecting never to hear another word about the house on the corner of Cottage and Fuller.

She was mistaken. Mrs. Hillman's heirs called the Edgartown real estate agent. Apparently, days before the old woman died, she had talked continuously about how Margaret must have the house. The family would sell it to her if she met the late homeowner's original price. With an eerie sense that old Mrs. Hillman had just concluded her side of the transaction, Margaret accepted.

After closing the deal, Margaret, her husband, and their four children spent several autumn weeks in their new abode. From the start everything seemed slightly amiss. For one thing, their normally lackadaisical cat turned psychotic.

From the moment they set it down in the dining room, it hissed, growled, and made strange rumbling noises. Its back arched and fur bristling, it would spring in a circle, landing squarely on all four paws. Margaret set the animal outside and it disappeared for three days, only to return covered with cobwebs as if it had spent the whole time cowering in a crawl space.

One night Margaret and her husband woke up to a terrific banging noise. Margaret glanced at the clock aglow on her night table. Both hands had fused into one hand on the twelve: Dead on midnight.

One evening their five-year-old son clambered down the stairs and appeared, trembling, in the front sitting room. He'd been awakened by a terrible knocking on the wall between his bedroom and the attic space on the second floor. Margaret was nonplussed. (Her son's room happened to be the one in which Mrs. Hillman had died.) Margaret, too, had heard the knocking but had tried to ignore it, explaining it away as some sort of nighttime quirk of old-fashioned construction: possibly beams settling against their supports.

Margaret's husband continued to resent this second home. In response, the young wife promised to return a profit. She arranged to rent the house for the following summer, finding a month-long set of tenants for July and then August. However, in mid-July, she found to her surprise and dismay that the tenants had decamped without warning.

It wasn't until the following Thanksgiving on the island that she learned the truth from her hairdresser: Their house had a ghost. Her husband learned it from the hardware store clerk. Everyone seemed to know about it except them.

The previous July, it turned out, the tenants' teen-aged son, alone in the house, had heard what sounded like a prowler upstairs. Alarmed, he called the police. Within minutes, a pair of squad cars appeared and several officers climbed the stairs to investigate the source of the disturbance. Two of the officers entered the cavernous attic space and shone their lights around. Nothing appeared to be out of order, and yet, when they turned to leave, they stepped back with a start. Although they'd left the door ajar, it was now closed and a cane was propped against it as if to bar their exit. If someone had played a trick on them, how could that person have possibly shut the door and positioned the cane without remaining in the room? The men were bothered by this conundrum and were further distressed to learn that the cane had belonged to old Mrs. Hillman, who had never been without it as she limped her way around the house.

Back at the police station, one of the officers, working on a hunch, checked the records: This strange episode occurred a year to the day that old Mrs. Hillman had died.

So, who was this strange person who cast a long posthumous shadow over her home? Actually there were two Mrs. Hillmans who had served as chatelaine of the house. The master of the manor had been Captain Horace Hillman, president of the Rod and Gun Club and destined to become a renowned fisherman throughout New England. (In the late 1920s he ironed a record thousand-pound broadbill swordfish.) In 1893 he married Henrietta Norton, a gracious and charitable lady whose abrupt decline and death in 1932 had surprised her wide circle of friends. If rumors of mysterious circumstances had surrounded her demise, they were further fueled when in the same year Captain Hillman married young Agnes Forman, who had grown up in the house across the street. (A waggish acquaintance at the time darkly intoned the line from *Hamlet*: "The funeral baked meats did coldly furnish forth the marriage table." Another acquaintance told Margaret Steele, "Horace Hillman was a very naughty man.")

Captain Hillman's son and daughter by his first wife were left unprotected by the unhappy fact that their mother predeceased their father. The famous fisherman was seemingly fonder of his new wife, his buddies, and his adoring fans than of his own offspring. This was evidenced when, in 1950, he died at home of a sudden heart attack at the age of seventy-nine and left his entire estate to the second Mrs. Hillman. One hundred dollars apiece went to his son and his daughter.

Perhaps shy to begin with, or else made sensitive by malicious gossip, the second Mrs. Hillman had from the start of her marriage remained a deeply private person. Little was known or remarked about her until her death in 1967, whereupon the *Vineyard Gazette* reported the unusual details of her will. Rather than rectify the injustice of her husband's legacy, she bequeathed one-third of her estate to her niece and two-thirds to her cousin in Falmouth (the same relatives who sold the house to Margaret).

When Margaret took possession of the Hillman house, therefore, she unwittingly stumbled into a witch's brew of family discontents. None of the living members ever gave her a moment's trouble, but of the departed Hillmans— well, the new homeowner soon learned that at least one of them appeared to have an ax to grind. But whether it was the first Mrs. Hillman who died in questionable circumstances, or the second Mrs. Hillman who had been forced to live with the consequences of her untimely engagement, or perhaps the amoral master mariner himself—whoever haunted the house at Cottage and Fuller apparently had a great deal of unfinished business to transact.

Margaret continued to hear disturbing accounts from her tenants. Colbert Smith, a writer and correspondent for the *Vineyard Gazette*, once stayed in the house. He wrote his landlady: "I don't believe in this kind of thing, but—" and what followed was a five-page, single-spaced letter detailing all the strange occurrences: the tapping on walls, footsteps, creakings, and the refusal of many of his guests to spend a night in the room in which Mrs. Hillman had died (not that any of them had known about the matter). To complicate things, his wife was expecting a baby, and her own bad case of jitters about the house necessitated cutting short their stay.

Finally, Margaret's own circumstances dictated she alter her second home into her primary one. She had divorced her husband and had brought her four children and their cat to live in what she now had to accept was the haunted house at the intersection of Cottage and Fuller Streets. The house's reputation was so widely known, in fact, that many social acquaintances refused invitations to dinner or even to drop-in visits.

For nearly ten years Margaret and her children lived with the inevitable signs of a ghostly intruder: creaking stairs, wall knockings, and an ongoing spooking of anyone who tried to pass the night in the guest bedroom. The first night Margaret heard the tinkling of the piano, she dismissed it as the work of the cat, but the next morning, as she prepared breakfast in the kitchen, she heard the creature meow at the back door, having been shut out all night. Whatever the disturbance, Margaret learned to dismiss it from her mind and she grew adept at providing ready explanations to her children to still their fears. And yet all of them knew in the bottom of their hearts that a ghost was as much a resident of their house as they were. Sometimes they offhandedly remarked, "There goes Mrs. Hillman again," then plowed back into their activities.

Then one night Margaret was awakened by a troubling sound downstairs: footsteps more pronounced than the ghost's now-familiar tread. She heard the front door open and bang shut, followed by the same loud report from the storm door. Clearly someone had gained access to the house and was now abruptly and none-too-subtly leaving! Scurrying to the front window, she heard the clomp of feet down the wide front steps and the sounds of someone running to the house across the street (the house in which Agnes Forman had grown up before marrying Captain Hillman). Margaret could see no one! All the same, a sense of violation stirred her to call the police, and once again two patrol cars arrived within minutes. They, too, could find no trace of a trespasser.

The event of that night marked the very last time Margaret's house entertained a ghost. "It was as if she very loudly and plainly took her leave," Margaret reported. And yet this same departure pointed in the direction of Mrs. Hillman's former home. Could the ghost have comfortably installed herself there? Today Margaret confides: "I've always wanted to ask the people who live there, but part of me is afraid to find out the truth. I might feel responsible for driving her to them!"

In the off-season, that other house on the corner of Cottage and Fuller Streets sits abandoned, its quaint steeples agleam with silvery snow, its dark windows featureless, unreadable. If Agnes Forman Hillman does reside there now, she faces the silent avenues without a single stir of a curtain or a murmur of sound to betray her presence.

16

House of Dark Shadows

IT SITS ALONE ON A WINDSWEPT PROMONTORY, looking south over the sea. With gabled windows, a steepled roofline, and wild roses growing in profusion over a crumbling stone wall, the Hartwig* homestead resembles anyone's notion of a dream cottage by the shore. Yet some of its inhabitants over the years would better define living there as a nightmare.

A former caretaker confided, "The things that go on in the house come in cycles. There was one summer when the ghost action got so rough, we couldn't get anyone to stay for a whole week's rental. Tenants would just up and leave in the middle of the night. Once the kitchen door was left standing open, as if the people had been chased out. After that, the place stood empty for a couple of years. It got to look sort of derelict."

In the past few summers, rentals have flourished again at the Hartwig homestead, but if you happen to cross paths with recent tenants, you discover strange events still unfold there. A young man who shared the house with several roommates reported, "We all had this same experience: In the middle of the night you'd wake up in a panic because it felt as if all your breath had been sucked out of you!"

Another tenant spoke of roving shapes on the walls. "Do you recall how when you were a child shadows used to scare you, so you'd look around to see what was causing them? Well, in the Hartwig place, you'd look around and nothing matched the patterns on the wall."

"I lived there with two other women one summer," said a woman with a seasonal business in Oak Bluffs. "Two of us immediately thought that the house was haunted. There was just a kind of depressed, weepy feeling to the place. But our third roommate said we were nuts. Then one night she came home long after the two of us had gone to bed. As she walked toward the house, she saw the silhouette of a female standing in the shadows behind the gate, just watching her. Then she heard a loud banging sound coming from the roof. She thought we'd staged things to scare her. The next morning at breakfast she was very upset with us, but when she saw our shocked expressions, she realized we hadn't had anything to do with it. It certainly reaffirmed our hunch that truly strange things went on there." After

*Names changed to protect confidentiality

that, the woman who related the story was careful never to spend a night alone in the house. "If I learned my room-mates would be out all night, I'd also stay away," she remarked, "even if it meant shooting pool until dawn with friends in Gay Head."

Yet another tenant, a young woman who worked at a restaurant in Menemsha, spoke of a summer when her various roommates at the homestead had a terrifying experience with the mirror in the upstairs bathroom. She said, "You'd be brushing your hair or something and just for a second you'd see a second face—the twisted face of a hairy guy with bloodshot eyes—staring at you behind your own reflection."

This same tenant described a somewhat comical night when a trio of friends came to visit from Buffalo, New York. "The other roommates and I treated them to stories about all the spooky stuff that had happened that summer. We got ourselves so worked up, we decided we'd all sleep in the same room that night. We were all too chicken to even brush our teeth alone, so in this big group we went from room to room and suitcase to suitcase to collect everything we needed before we settled down with blankets in the living room. And we kept all the lights on!"

What influences from the past have caused these deep disturbances in the Hartwig homestead? It could be fiction or it could be fact, but everyone familiar with the house repeats the same story: Many generations ago on the property, a young girl fell into a well and drowned. It's her mother's unhappiness—the mother also long dead now—that permeates the tangy sea air. Another explanation comes from a psychic who stayed in the house a few years ago. Acutely sensitive to the melancholy that fairly dripped from the eaves, the psychic experienced a deep intuition that the ghost of a young woman roamed the promontory searching for a young husband who had died at sea. The psychic said the bride existed in a ghostly limbo wherein she had no awareness of either her husband's demise or her own. Accordingly, the psychic stood alone on the bluff to commune with the desolate spirit, apprising it of the facts. After that, apparently, peace reigned over the Hartwig manor, though it's obvious to more recent tenants that restless entities have risen again to walk the fog-bound cliffs.

A mother of three who rented the house for the month of September felt the strong presence of poltergeists. "I guess I mean poltergeists," she murmured, "sort of obnoxious spirits, right? When we arrived, I unpacked a box of new, fluffy, very expensive red bath towels. I set them down on the kitchen table, then went upstairs to make the beds. When I returned to the kitchen, the towels were gone. Naturally, I accused every member of the family but everyone stared back at me blankly. I turned that house upside down and finally had to buy some more towels in Vineyard Haven. Then, on the last day of our stay, I went down into the cellar to switch off the hot water and there were my red towels stacked neatly on an old beat-up chest!"

The same woman complained that things went missing during her entire vacation; sometimes for minutes, sometimes for days, but invariably she would find the delinquent object, usually in a spot conspicuously normal and out in the open; a spot she'd visually scoured many times over.

Can anything be done about this property deemed by some "the most haunted house on the island"? On being asked this question, a local psychic familiar with the house was skeptical about any long-term improvements. "It's one of those intersections of the spirit world," she observed,

"where supernatural crosscurrents keep wafting through."
Should people go on living there, then, if only for a week at
a time? The psychic grinned and said, "We've all lived with
worse crises than having our towels stashed in the cellar."

17

Intimations of
Immortality

NURSE, A DOCTOR, AND A PATIENT who was
destined to die. These constituted the cast of
players brought together to enact a mysterious drama one summer evening at Martha's
Vineyard Hospital in Oak Bluffs.

Shirley Hugger had worked as a nurse on Martha's
Vineyard for fourteen years. A deeply intuitive person, she
enjoyed her forays across fields and shore. Sometimes these
treks enlivened her with a sense of communing with spirits. "Last summer I was beachcombing around Wasque on

Chappaquiddick," she reports, "and I had this irresistible urge to find an arrowhead. I'd never come across one before, but I knew that if I did I would feel closer to our Indian heritage." She sat on the sand, closed her eyes, and fell into a meditative trance. Soon she sensed an overpowering presence standing a few feet away from her. Opening her eyes, she glanced over her left shoulder to the spot where she knew beyond the shadow of a doubt an invisible Native American gazed back at her. Rising and stumbling forward, she saw something glowing pewter-gray on the ground halfway between her and the presence. It was an arrowhead.

On the night shift at the hospital, Shirley's extrasensory abilities have helped her attend dying patients with compassion. She explained, "Sometimes they fight it, but you know when the time is right to tell them it's okay to let go." On other occasions, however, when death snatches someone with the stealth of a ninja warrior, Shirley has difficulty relinquishing the patient to that good night.

On one warm August evening, a sixty-year-old man, who looked twenty years younger, arrived at the hospital with vague symptoms of heart trouble: shallow breathing and some pain, but nothing that kept him from hobnobbing with old acquaintances. Slim, trim, and endearingly boyish for his age, the man had lived on the island for many years before moving to the mainland. A crafts fair in West Tisbury had brought him back for a joyous reunion with friends and favorite haunts.

"He was in great spirits, despite his discomfort," said Shirley. "His leather-tooled items had sold out at his booth and he'd even had the opportunity to give President Clinton one of his belts! While he was with us, he called his ex-wife on the mainland to tell her about his success at the fair. It was almost incidental that he happened to have landed in the hospital."

Meanwhile Dr. Michael Jacobs carefully monitored the patient's progress. Suddenly everything went haywire as the patient tripped pell-mell into a full-scale heart attack. Michael, Shirley, and the other staff flew into action. They attached an intravenous drip, gave him morphine and nitroglycerin, applied the oxygen and the electrical connections, and, finally, as his heartbeat became slower and slower, resorted to the defibrillator. But it was of no use. The patient hurtled headlong toward death.

Michael later observed, "He was 'trying to die.' That's an expression we use in the medical profession. It has nothing to do with a death wish or suicide or anything like that. It simply means there's a turning point in a patient's struggle where all arrows point in one direction only. As a doctor, you can feel yourself losing the battle against this fundamental motion."

In folklore and legend, humankind has found other ways of expressing this final abduction: the Grim Reaper, appointment in Samara, the angel of death, the Stygian shore. However we conceive of this unavoidable passing, we humbly acknowledge that when death decides to take us, it will take us, and no back chat. There are no appeals to a higher court.

But on this particular night in the confines of the emergency room at the Martha's Vineyard Hospital, Shirley and Michael looked upon their lost patient with grief in their hearts. "Only a short time before," said Shirley, "he'd been so alive, so animated! We just had a really hard time giving him up."

The body lay lifeless on the table. A sheet was drawn over it and, one by one, the emergency staff filed out of the room. Michael marched morosely to his office, leaving Shirley to mourn over the corpse.

Alone at his desk, Michael began to fill out the necessary forms. With his pen poised, however, he found himself unable to continue. Some compelling urge dragged him from his desk, and, in a sort of benumbed stupor, he staggered back to the emergency room. As he entered, he saw another nurse had joined Shirley and the two of them were tugging at the window sash. The window sprang free to admit a gentle night breeze and the sounds of seaside insect life.

Suddenly all three people in the room experienced a whispery motion of air coming from the direction of the dead patient. A sound like softly-flapping wings rose from the table and rustled toward the open window. The drapery luffed with the breeze of this strange interior cyclone, then sagged, then luffed, then sagged again. Whatever strange combustion of atmosphere had filled the room passed swiftly into the night breeze. All was quiet in the hospital again. The drapes hung motionless against the wall. The corpse lay undisturbed.

Michael, unwilling to believe what he'd seen with his own eyes, and heard with his own ears, asked almost rhetorically, "Why did you open the window?"

Shirley replied with a shrug, "To set his spirit free." Then she switched off the lights and they turned their gaze to the bright northern sky where the stars twinkled as they received their new pinpoint of light.

18

Forty Days and Forty Nights

ORN BEFORE WORLD WAR I, their lives played out like the plot of an Edith Wharton novel. Handsome, talented, and rich, Marietta and Louise Crawford* were twin sisters from New York. Although independent in their professional lives—Marietta was a sculptor and Louise one of America's first female stage managers—they never managed to throw off the yoke of their father's domestic tyranny. In earlier years, Mr. Crawford managed to foil his daughters' efforts to become engaged, fearing, it was rumored, that the family fortune would be dissipated by husbands and offspring. With his patriarchal grip on the financial leash, he forced the twins to live with their parents, both in their winter mansion in New Jersey and in their spacious captain's house on South Summer Street in Edgartown. Thus it was that Marietta and Louise were destined to spend the whole of their lives together, then to die only a year apart, and, quite possibly, become inseparable ghosts in their own summer house.

In their early eighties, the sisters' failing health prompted them to hire Mrs. Joan Kendall* to look after them. Mrs. Kendall tended the sisters and their house for nearly twenty years and knew them intimately. "They were characters, those two!" she said as she reminisced about them several years after their deaths. "They squabbled all the time. They never had the chance to make their own lives. When their father was alive, he'd take them traveling around the world, but he let them know he'd disinherit them if they even thought about leasing their own apartments."

Presumably, once their parents died, Marietta and Louise found their living arrangements too entrenched a habit to break. Then in 1990, Marietta died of a heart attack and was buried in an Edgartown cemetery, several blocks away from her home. Within a year, Louise's health failed miserably, and Mrs. Kendall, under a doctor's supervision, nursed her around the clock. One day the remaining twin closed her eyes, fell into a deep sleep, and without any sort of fuss or obvious discomfort, passed away.

The faithful nurse had promised the sisters she would stay in their home until all legal matters were settled and the luxurious furniture and antiques were cataloged and carted

---

*Names changed to protect confidentiality

away by the auction houses. A few days after Louise's funeral, as Mrs. Kendall sat reading a book in the front parlor, she felt a vibration run through the floor and her rocking chair. The entire house began to quake. She could hear the walls creak and the windows rattle. Suddenly, overhead, it sounded as if a herd of elephants were lumbering from room to room as fresh temblors rocked the foundation. Terrified, Mrs. Kendall listened to the shrill tinkling of all the antique glassware in the cabinets. Then, just when she thought the ceiling was about to cave in on her, the shaking abruptly ceased. Evening silence descended back over the house.

"The same thing happened every night around eight o'clock," Mrs. Kendall recalled. "After a while it got so you could set your watch by it. The house would roll and rumble, that pounding sound would boom out overhead, and then it would be over. Even though I learned to cope with it, I never walked around to see what was happening. I'd just freeze in the rocking chair and wait it out."

Mrs. Kendall confined most of her activities to the downstairs front parlor, where she tucked in for the night on the day bed. On one of those occasions, just as she was falling into the first stages of a drowse, she felt the mattress depress at the edge of the bed, as if someone were sitting there beside her. Turning with a start, she saw, from the pale street lamp light filtering in through the bay windows, that she was perfectly alone. "That happened a lot," she affirmed later. "I got used to that, too."

Once late at night she saw a radiant white light float from one end of the downstairs hallway to the other, finally disappearing into the front door. Sometimes she heard the low babble of conversation issuing from another room, but when she ambled over to check, she would find no one there. Other times the door between the front parlor and the foyer would close by itself.

One day when Mrs. Kendall needed to travel off-island, her younger son arrived to look after the house in her stead. "He felt the eight o'clock earthquake and saw the moving light, but what really upset him was when he saw Louise herself move through the front parlor, pushing her walker ahead of her. He never offered to relieve me again," she said with a chuckle.

Her older son also experienced a strange incident. Once when he accompanied his mother on an errand in the upstairs rooms, he glanced down at his arm to see a line of blood trickling from a long scratch. He had no idea how he'd incurred the superficial, yet dramatic-looking, injury.

At last, Mrs. Kendall grew jittery about remaining in the house. She wanted to honor her promise to the twins and yet wondered how long her nerves could stand the haunting. The lawyers and auction houses were taking their time and she knew she could never tell them to speed things up because the Crawford ghosts annoyed her. Instead, over a coffee klatch with the Caribbean-born housekeeper next door, she poured out her troubles.

The housekeeper listened with sympathy and, in her lilting dialect said, "Happens back home all the time. After a burial sometimes, spirits get all riled up. They walk around, bust things, pull the bedcovers off you in the middle of the night. What we do is, we go to the pharmacist. He prepares something to help us sleep."

"Well, I'm not taking sleeping pills!" objected Mrs. Kendall.

The housekeeper nodded sagely. "No need to. Time's almost up."

"What do you mean?" asked Mrs. Kendall.

"Forty days and forty nights," the woman announced with impressive conviction. "That's how long it takes for the spirits to calm down. After that you'll have no trouble."

Mrs. Kendall kept her eye on the calendar. Sure enough, on the fortieth day following the anniversary of Louise Crawford's death, the house settled down. No more 8:00 P.M. elephant herds stomping overhead, no more rattling of antique glass, no more bed sittings or roving lights or closing doors or apparitions. The Crawford twins had passed over into the next realm, perhaps to reside with their parents, perhaps not. It would be comforting to think that family dysfunction, like everything else, must finally end, even if, in the afterworld, it takes forty days and forty nights to allow it to rest in peace.

19

Parlez-Vous Death?

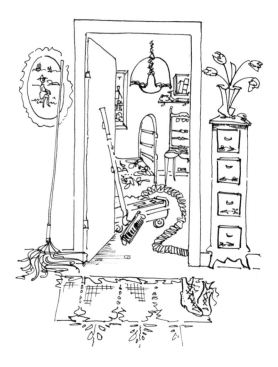

I N THE BEGINNING it was just another cleaning job. Located in a historic district of one of the down-island towns, the charming, white-clapboard, black-shuttered whaling captain's home looked to Marianne Evans* like the most pleasant abode imaginable. Alone in the house in the bright light of day, she decided to tackle the downstairs first, working back to front.

She set the vacuum cleaner down in the center of the spacious rear bedroom that faced the late springtime garden. Instantly she had the creepy sensation that someone was watching her. Glancing around nervously, she spotted no one in the room or in the garden; besides, the stare seemed to be generated much closer to hand, as if someone hovered, breathed almost, right over her. Although it was a warm day, goose bumps rose on her arms. Without hesitation, she plucked up the vacuum cleaner and walked briskly out of the room. She would deal with it later. Much later.

Hours after, with the rest of the house spic and span, including the library whose leatherbound volumes Marianne had lovingly dusted and straightened on their shelves, the young woman was ready to address the troublesome downstairs bedroom. Once again she strode in with her vacuum cleaner, determined to ignore whatever malevolent presence stalked the chamber. To her dismay, the sensation of being watched returned with a vengeance. Working quickly, she plugged in the appliance. When she stooped to turn it on, the overhead light flicked off. Annoyed, she crossed over to the light switch and snapped it on again, then returned to the vacuum. The light extinguished itself once more, and, at the same time, the door slammed shut.

Marianne gave out a little squeal. Wasting no more time, she turned on the vacuum cleaner and applied it to the carpet. Over the thrum of the machine, she thought she heard a man's voice mumbling in her ear. Convinced she had to be imagining things, she started to hum a favorite hymn. Undeterred, the male voice spoke more audibly, and now Marianne could recognize the disembodied speech was being delivered in French!

Although the words sounded familiar, she had no idea what they meant; her high-school French had left her ill-

---

*Names changed to protect confidentiality

equipped to speak or understand anything more than directions to the metro. But she began to detect a pattern. Whatever the presence was saying, he intoned it over and over again—some sort of a chant or a prayer.

Marianne felt as much challenged as frightened, and now, to overpower the spirit—or whatever it was—she abandoned her low hum and rendered her hymn with gusto. The presence countered by shouting his words in her ear. At the same time, Marianne began to see, on the periphery of her vision, a tall man in uniform. This was too much for her, and, seizing the vacuum cleaner, she yanked the plug from the wall socket and fled the room.

Once she was out of the bedroom, every sensation of haunting ceased. The silence and the untrammeled atmosphere of the rest of the house only intensified Marianne's sense of a troubled realm in the rear bedroom. She quickly stowed the vacuum cleaner and prepared to leave. Passing through the foyer, she glanced through the open door to the library and stopped, startled. Earlier she had left the room in perfect order, but now she saw that one of the books poked from the shelf as if someone had examined it and replaced it without aligning it properly. Mystified, she entered the room and took the stray volume in her hands. It was a history of World War II fighter pilots. Was the ghost trying to identify himself?

Arriving home that afternoon, Marianne related the events of her excursion into the supernatural to her husband. Benjamin,* who spoke perfect French, listened to his wife's version of the ghost's prayer; something she'd heard repeated enough times to reproduce phonetically. "Mere Marie, priez pour nous maintenant et à l'heure de notre morte." Benjamin translated, "Mother Mary, pray for us now and at the hour of our death."

Marianne heard the words and shuddered. The morbid prayer only heightened her sense of the spirit's macabre frame of mind. She was determined to never again clean the house alone. She would drag whomever she could— her husband or a friend—along with her. Her kindly nature told her the ghost was reaching out for help of some sort. The key seemed to lie in his identity, or perhaps the circumstances surrounding his death. Had he been shot down over France during the war, perhaps? She knew she ought to make an effort to relieve him of the quandary or eternal disorientation in which he appeared to be trapped, but she simply hadn't the stamina to face up to his depressing presence on her own again.

Over the summer, Marianne stuck to the plan to bring along a companion. Never again was she plagued by the same sense of bombardment in the rear bedroom. But, from time to time, the ghost did remind her of his continuing preoccupation with the house. Once, when a dog next door kept up a ceaseless, obnoxious yapping, Marianne glanced over the fence to see a heavy broom disengage itself from the wall and topple over to the ground, missing the dog by inches. The young woman broke out laughing— perhaps the ghost wasn't such a darkly brooding spirit after all.

A coincidence in my own research brought me back to this same house. That August following Marianne's adventure, I received a telephone call from some off-islanders visiting for a couple of weeks. They'd heard I conducted a walking tour involving ghosts and wondered if I'd be interested in their experiences in the home they had rented for their short stay. It turned out to be the very address of the French-speaking soldier.

Their first night in the house, asleep in the upstairs

master bedroom, the couple had been roused by the sound of a huge crash downstairs, very much as if a large chandelier had come loose from the ceiling and had smashed onto the hardwood floor. Leaping from bed, they had raced downstairs to survey the damage. Nothing was amiss in the ground-floor rooms. Every hanging lamp rested undisturbed and not a single shard of anything breakable could be found. Thoroughly mystified, the couple had returned to bed. They might even have forgotten about the alarming pseudo-smash were it not for the fact that the same nerve-jangling noise occurred night after night. By the end of their stay, they had learned to nod in groggy acknowledgment and fall back to sleep.

One other event took place in those two weeks. The husband's mother had come to stay, and they'd graciously fixed up the rear bedroom for her—that airy chamber with its soothing views of the neatly landscaped yard. In the middle of the night—a warm, balmy, August evening—the woman had awakened shivering with cold. "It was like a meat locker in there," she'd reported over breakfast the next morning. Her son and daughter-in-law had offered to move her to a bedroom upstairs but she'd declined. She too had heard the nighttime sound of the smashing chandelier and between that and the sepulchrally cold guest room, she decided to cut her visit short.

Personally, I know a number of people who would find a guest room of this sort a useful addition to the house, particularly toward the end of summer when Vineyarders have been set upon by about twenty visitors too many!

20

Another Piece of the Chappaquiddick Puzzle

ABOUT THE KENNEDY/KOPECHNE TRAGEDY at Dyke Bridge on Chappaquiddick, virtually every angle has been scrutinized: what time the couple left the party, who had been driving, how much liquor had been consumed, how Ted Kennedy had managed to escape, why the phone number for the rescue squad had failed to transmit from the senator's brain to his dialing finger, how long Mary Jo may or may not have survived in a hypothetical bubble of trapped air; these questions and a hundred others have been sifted by the judicial system, the press, and the public like a Vineyard sandbar probed for quahogs. The event has entered the realm of history's great and classic mysteries, never solved, and therefore perennially a subject of debate, speculation, and, unhappily, posthumous gossip.

Into this morass of theories and imponderables, I would like to add one more dimension to the events of the night of July 18, 1969, and that is, of course, the element of the supernatural. Whatever drunken revels or misbegotten reunion the six men and six women of the Kennedy/Kopechne party had blundered into, to their horrible luck must be added the further complication of conducting their socializing within the bounds of the most haunted terrain of an already ghost-infested island.

"Chappaquiddick is a spiritual haven," asserted writer and occult specialist Nelson Ross,* in a recent phone conversation. "All my experiments and studies over Chappaquiddick's hills and hollows have convinced me that nowhere else will you find such a high concentration of ectoplasmic activity."

Ghost stories from Chappy, as the Vineyard's little cousin island is known, abound. Tucked behind the northern shore, Squaw Hollow go its name from the woman's screams heard over the wind on moonless nights. The cries re-create, or so the legend goes, a long-ago evening when an Indian male slashed his wife to death with a hatchet. Overlooking Katama Bay, in an old whaling captain's house, a handyman of a ghost methodically shifts carpenter's tools from table to bench to cabinet. Along Litchfield Road at night, strange lights have danced in the woods. People with clairvoyant sensibilities have reported an unease stealing

---

*Some names changed to protect confidentiality

over them if they chance to linger on Chappy past four in the afternoon, necessitating a speedy departure, although many others are attracted to the little island for the spiritual tonic bestowed on them from the very air they breathe there.

Even the cottage where the fateful Kennedy party took place has received a spooky rating. John McSweeny, who leased the small two-bedroom house and the still smaller studio across the yard several years after the accident, experienced a dose of unexplainable agitation the entire time he lived there. "It was nerve-wracking to begin with, because people were still coming around to peek in the windows of the 'Kennedy party house,'" he told me recently. "But beyond that, I felt that the cottage was riddled with ghosts. At night you would hear moaning sounds above the wind. I'd hear something moving around in the attic, and one night the chimney caught fire.

"I had a Swedish ivy plant on the kitchen sill, and its leaves grew so big that people would freak out when they saw it. It was an honest-to-God botanical mutant. On the morning I was set to move out, the plant fell and crashed in the sink. That same day, I climbed the pull-out ladder to the attic, poked my head through the opening, and, even though the space was completely bare, I thanked the ghosts for letting me escape unharmed."

So it's not inconceivable the atmosphere of the Kennedy cookout was subtly influenced by watchful, perhaps mischievous, shades who existed, if they could be said to exist at all, for the purpose of causing small, manageable amounts of havoc. At any rate, at some point in the evening—Ted Kennedy maintained it was 11:30 P.M., though Deputy Sheriff Christopher Look placed the time of the infamous ride at 12:35 A.M.—the senator and the secretary left the party, climbed into a dark Oldsmobile, drove about half a mile down the main road, and turned right onto what's colloquially known as Dyke Road, and sometimes less commonly referred to as Cemetery Road.

This rough, bumpy lane runs about half a mile along a large tract of land called Tom's Neck Farm, one of the most fabulously haunted rural spots in all of New England. Island raconteur Milton Jeffers (see "One For the [Other World] Road," page 60) supplied a wealth of information when he told me of his boyhood growing up near the farm: "When I was a kid, back in the 1930s, we heard that some workmen up at Tom's Neck near Poucha Pond, were laying in post holes when they uncovered a human skeleton. Dr. Clement Nevin arrived to check it out, and he said it was an Indian who died in the eighteenth century. Two arrowheads were lodged in the rib bones. A couple of weeks later, my father and I came across the remains, still lying out there in a box. My father, who was almost six feet tall, lifted them up and we saw that the skeleton was a lot taller than he was! About six-foot-six! That was some large Indian! Over the years, I've heard of other human bones excavated on the land."

Milton Jeffers's father spoke of the time when, a young lad himself, he'd strolled past three Indians sitting calmly on the cedar split-rail fence that once bordered Tom's Neck Farm. Clad in feathers and buckskin and passing a pipe around, the three were clearly apparitions from the past, for the eyewitness, a Native American himself, had never seen anyone he knew in the "modern age," circa 1890, dressed that way. Milton recalls, "He kept walking, then shook his head and circled back. The three men were still there! He went home, fretted about the whole thing, then returned for a third peek. The three ancient Indians still sat on the fence, passing the pipe. My father jogged home and went straight to bed!"

Only a couple of years ago, an Edgartown mason we'll call Simon Thiese encountered another brand of ghostly doings at Tom's Neck. Working alone at the farmhouse, the workman arrived the first morning to find a closet door wide open. Without paying it any heed, he closed it. The second morning he found the door open again, so again he closed it, but this time the minor phenomenon kept preying on his mind. On the third morning, discovering the door once again sprung wide, he not only shut it tight, but bent the latch to ensure that nothing could get it to budge open again. Perhaps not surprisingly at this point, on the fourth morning, the door again stood open. This time the mason furiously nailed it shut and it stayed shut through the duration of his work on the farmhouse.

During the mason's stint at Tom's Neck, something else occurred to disturb his peace of mind. One day as he labored over the fireplace, he detected the scent of a woman's perfume. Glancing all around, he could find no female presence to account for the smell, and yet his nose alone told him the source of the fragrance had to be close at hand. Finally the assault on his olfactory nerves grew so strong as to be almost unbearable, and the mason demanded that his unseen stalker clear out. The scent abruptly vanished.

Milton Jeffers recalled one more story about Tom's Neck, this one also transpiring in his father's long-ago boyhood. "He was walking alone at night down the Dyke Road, and suddenly this big light flashed all around him, illuminating everything as if it were the middle of the day!" (See "Vintage Vinyardiana," page 134, regarding the Katama Money Light.) Milton continued, "He was so scared, he bolted for home, and he never walked that way alone at night again."

The drowning of Mary Jo Kopechne wasn't, in fact, the first mysterious fatality to take place in the environs of Tom's Neck Farm. In 1904, the owner of the property, an affluent forty-three-year-old farmer named Charles M. Pease, surprised friends and neighbors when, without warning, he returned from an off-island expedition with a beautiful twenty-something bride. Little was known about the young woman other than that she was a schoolteacher of Swedish descent. Four days after the newlyweds appeared, Farmer Pease was found dead at the edge of a grove on his own property. He'd been shot through the mouth. A .44-caliber rifle lay a few feet from him. Suicide was ruled out when the medical examiner determined that, with the barrel positioned in the man's mouth, it would have been physically impossible for the deceased to reach the trigger. Local law enforcement advanced the theory that a jealous suitor of the bride's had tracked the newlyweds to the island, murdered the middle-aged groom, and neatly escaped on a boat anchored close to shore. Although no evidence arose to support the existence of this third party, the case was closed without ever having been tried. The beautiful and mysterious young widow sold the farm and left the island infinitely richer than when she'd arrived a short time previously.

The death of Charles Pease cast a pall over the little island of Chappaquiddick, and certainly over Tom's Neck Farm, for quite a long while. In later years, some of the ghost tales of the region were handily attributed to the luckless bridegroom. People who had known him were disconcerted when they spotted the late farmer roaming fields and coves.

Later, Harry McGinty,* a reclusive caretaker of one

of the huge summer homes along the southern Chappaquiddick shore, related his own specific sighting of the
alleged Farmer Pease ghost.

Half a century-ago, recalled McGinty, an actual
wooden dike on Poucha Pond had kept the saltwater estu-
ary separate from a freshwater feeding ground for ducks and
geese. Harry, then a boy of seventeen, was hiding behind a
blind at dawn to hunt these same fowl. Suddenly, without
Harry having any idea where he could have come from, a
man sprouted up between him and his game. He described
the figure as being of medium height, around forty or fifty
years of age, and garbed in his dark-suited Sunday best.
Although Chappy harbored fewer than twenty year-round
residents in those days, Harry had never so much as
glimpsed the man before. He added, "He glared at me as
if I were trespassing. At any rate, I had this strong impression he didn't approve of me being there, doing what I
was doing. I skedaddled plenty fast. I was young and easily
cowed back then. Nowadays I probably would've shot him
along with the damn birds."

So how to blend this bounty of supernatural material
with the Kennedy/Kopechne tragedy? To assist me in my
efforts, I contacted a young Edgartown psychic known
locally for her success in sniffing out historical tidbits beyond the limits of formal records that are later uncannily
substantiated by oral accounts of old-timers. On a cold
day in early spring, Christina* and I set out for the
Kennedy/Kopechne trail of tears. The Chappy ferry was
temporarily closed to autos in order to replace the old
wharves, so we journeyed across the five hundred feet of
water as foot-passengers, our bicycles at the ready. As we
biked the three-and-a-half miles to the cottage an eerie
quiet accompanied us on this auto-free, off-season day. We

glided past leafless woods, seaside meadows, and open pastures, the only two creatures at large on the island.

Christina was amazed at the relative shabbiness of the notorious cottage. I realized that in the popular imagination, the Kennedy party could only have taken place in some glamorous, sprawling villa, as it might have done in a movie version. But no, the gray-shingled, single-story abode with its trim of peeling white paint looked almost ramshackle. We peered in the windows at two tiny bedrooms and the minuscule living room abutting the compact kitchen, all four rooms containing furniture that could only be described as plain in the extreme. Doubtless the cottage had appeared more upscale twenty-five years ago. Writing in 1976, Robert Sherrill, author of *The Last Kennedy*, described the place as "one of the nicest little cottages on Chappaquiddick . . . it went for $200 a week even in 1969."

On the lawn between the cottage and the studio, Christina spread out her paraphernalia on a red silk scarf. Nearby a crop of crocuses poked from the semi-frozen ground, all of the buds yellow except for one exquisite lavender blossom. With wan sunlight on our faces, we burned conifer-scented smudge sticks to drive away evil spirits. Christina recited ancient Celtic incantations and treated herself to whiffs of cedar incense, which normally facilitates her free-associative dream states. Nothing remotely dreamy seemed to suggest itself.

After a while we circled both dwellings with the smoky smudge stick. Christina was drawn much more strongly to the studio than the cottage. At the steps to the screened porch, she stooped and poked in the dead leaves with an implement resembling a feathered comb. "Someone lost a ring here a long time ago," she muttered, half to herself. I tried to distract her by suggesting another tour of the grounds, but repeatedly she returned to the steps and raked through the leaves. The air grew chilly, and I became slightly annoyed that we were wasting our time, but still she insisted on compulsively prodding around the steps. I heard her murmur, "Can't find my ring. Where is it?"

Finally, I realized Christina had fallen under the spell of someone else's monomania. Mary Jo's? I asked. Christina shook her head absently; she had difficulty determining whose long-ago loss she'd tapped into. "There's nothing here," she announced at last. "I detect an echo of Mary Jo, but she has nothing to tell us on this spot."

"Do you think she might be more forthcoming at Dyke Bridge?"

Christina held the cedar incense under her nose. "Maybe," was all she could safely volunteer.

The shadows had lengthened and the air was uncomfortably cold as we bicycled back along the main road to the famous T-junction where Deputy Sheriff Look had spotted, long past midnight, two, possibly three, figures in a dark Oldsmobile. We turned right on the dirt road that wends its way past Tom's Neck Farm to Poucha Pond.

Christina rode well ahead of me, and as we thumped and bumped our way to the water, I had no idea the psychic was reliving that fateful car ride on a long-ago July night. The minute we parked our bikes and stood before the dismantled bridge, I knew the atmosphere had dramatically changed.

Freezing wind gusted against our faces as Christina poured out her impressions, her gaze fixed on the channel's flowing gray-green water: "They fought all the way down the road. Many things had been bothering her. She'd had a recent abortion, so lately she'd been furious to learn Ted's wife was four months pregnant. At the party they were reconciled, but now her panic and anger returned. Ted shouted back at her, she shoved him a few times, he shoved her back. More shouting. He's driving, she doesn't see the bridge, she doesn't see anything, but Ted yells, 'Who's that?!' The car swerves, it flies a long way, flips over. Water. Water rushes in. . . . She still loves him. She wants him to know she forgives him."

(As a point of interest, I had waited to explain her "mission" on Chappy to Christina until the moment we embarked on the ferry. So without an opportunity to bone up on the events, and professing relative ignorance about the whole affair, she nonetheless correctly identified the south side of the bridge where the Oldsmobile had landed and the fact that it had stayed airborne farther than is commonly believed: I double-checked this with the diver—our own versatile John Farrar, who appears in several other chapters—who extricated Mary Jo's body from the car.)

We peddled away in silence. I wondered if anything about the event had been clarified, and I also ruminated over Christina's assertion that Ted had cried 'Who's that?!' before the car careened from the bridge. Had a ghostly entity from Tom's Neck Farm perhaps materialized at the worst moment possible—the spirit of Charles Pease, murdered groom, or a trio of ancient Indians? Or perhaps an unearthly flash of light? No one can say for certain, but this I do know: In the twenty operating years of Dyke Bridge, many cars had traversed it, with many drivers in varying states of sobriety and inebriation, but never before had a vehicle skidded over the admittedly flimsy rails. Perhaps on that moonless night Ted and Mary Jo—forlorn, drunk, exhausted, and in the grip of a quarrel, clipping along a godforsaken dirt road at anywhere from twenty to forty miles an hour toward a brittle and unseen bridge spanning a channel of swift, dark waters—perhaps this ill-fated couple were given one extra little nudge or shock or fleeting ambush by a phantom figure from Chappaquiddick's twilight zone.

Knowing the bewitching little island as I do, I'm here to say the theory I've advanced is considerably less daft than so many of the others that have floated around in the aftermath of the Chappaquiddick disaster.

21
Vintage Vinyardiana

A FEW LEGENDS AND ITEMS OF LORE have floated about Martha's Vineyard so persistently over the years that no ghost book would be complete without mentioning them.

The first involves the strangest front yard in all of New England. Located adjacent to the Mayhew Parsonage on South Water Street, wedged between the sidewalk and a pleasant white house facing the harbor, a family plot of ancient gravestones stares at the casual passer-by. Tipped either forward, backward, or sideways, the dark slate relics salute the street with inscriptions almost thoroughly obliterated by 350 years of wind and rain.

Eight of the earliest island Mayhews are reckoned to be buried here. Only three of the tablets are even remotely legible but archeologists believe all the deceased are close kith and kin of Governor Thomas Mayhew, who in 1642 purchased Martha's Vineyard, Nantucket, and the Elizabeth Islands for the grand total of forty pounds, sterling. The governor himself and his second wife, Jane, are believed to repose under a small, nondescript rock still closer to the street than the tombstones. On my walking tours, I love to mention this fact whenever stragglers chance to seat themselves above old Tom and Jane; the grave-squatters certainly levitate from the spot in a hurry!

Although no ghost stories connected with the monuments have ever been corroborated, some Vineyarders believe the very existence of the graves accounts for the many hauntings along the harbor-hugging lane. Based on my own research into the supernatural, I believe the untrammeled tombs pose no threat whatsoever since it is only from desecrated remains that problems arise. Earlier I've mentioned that the ransacking of Native American graves has been blamed for Edgartown's profusion of ghosts, but the resting ground of these earliest of white colonists has benefited by the higher regard succeeding white settlers have bestowed upon their own holdings.

You might think that over the years at least one of the homeowners next door to the Mayhew Parsonage has contemplated excavating the bones to make way for, say, a plot of hydrangeas, or a border of purple alyssum around a ceramic birdbath. And although the graves are protected by laws, statutes, and historical societies, ways and means could conceivably be found for transferring the aged coffins to a proper cemetery. For the sake of controlling the ghost activity in Edgartown, it's lucky no one has ever attempted this.

From Nova Scotia, an old story has made the rounds about a dead woman exhumed, on the evening following her funeral, by three young men intent on stealing her diamond ring. After they pried open the coffin and slipped the ring from her finger, they saw, by the light of the moon, the deceased stir as if from a deep sleep and then sit up! One of the men died on the spot from sheer fright. Another spent the rest of his days in a straitjacket in a mental hospital. The third lived to tell the tale. Meanwhile the woman got up and proceeded to walk home, where her family was obliged to admit her. She lived an eerie half-life for three more years, never speaking, never smiling, rarely straying from a corner in which she sat eyeing the others with a vacant stare. Then she died again and was buried for good.

It's doubtful that, if disinterred, old Thomas Mayhew, deceased for three hundred years, would sit up and ask which way to Dock Street. But, judging from the plethora of ghost stories arising from disrupted graves, the landowners of the family plot on South Water Street have rendered a service to the community by maintaining these unorthodox ornaments with the care and respect they deserve.

Another Vineyard oddity, a phenomenon with science fiction overtones, is the Katama Money Light. All along the Edgartown Great Plains, sightings have been reported numerous times over the past 150 years. On May 21, 1881, the *Vineyard Gazette* reported a glimpse of the Money Light by Enoch C. Cornell of Edgartown and a companion, out trawling the midnight waters of Caleb's Pond herring fishery on Chappaquiddick Island.

The paper summed up Mr. Cornell's experience as follows: "Looking across the harbor in a southwesterly direction, there appeared midway of the plain an apparently well-defined, square-edged shaft of red-hot iron, which issued from the ground and ascended for about half a mile, at which elevation it remained for the space of about two seconds, and then vanished without explosion or other manifestation. In about three or four seconds, a second shaft, a perfect duplicate of the former, appeared, differing only in that it went up less than two-thirds as high as the other, vanishing as before."

In the next century, another Edgartownian, Edward T. Vincent, encountered a similar sight on a night he and some fishing buddies anchored in Katama Bay off the shore of South Beach in Edgartown. He related the event to a reporter who filed this story in the *Vineyard Gazette*: "From the deck of the boat, Mr. Vincent looked over toward the woods and saw what many Great Plains people had seen before him, the strange light dancing above the dark woods. Twice it appeared, a ball of fire zigzagging above the trees, and twice it disappeared." Mr. Vincent confessed to a lack of surprise about the spectacle, having already heard firsthand accounts from his mother and his grandfather. His father, Samuel Warren Vincent, had theorized that the light was caused by the phosphorescence of decaying wood. A more fanciful explanation derived from the farmers of the region, who believed a pirate treasure had once been buried in the woods of Katama and, from time to time, this same supernatural light burned to disclose its location. Hence the name: Katama Money Light.

The last official sighting was recorded by two Edgartown policemen stationed at the town loading dock in the summer of 1974. But who's to say that in the last twenty years others haven't glimpsed it, from yachtsmen to midnight beachcombers to weekenders out late at night poking the dying embers of their barbecue grills? If they chanced to glance in the sky and see a bright shaft of red-hot light, they might have dismissed it as the result of too much sun and one too many beers.

The Scrubby Neck Witch is another old tale, this one dating from circa 1790 at the dawn of the golden age of whaling. Sailors in those days tended to be a superstitious lot. Perhaps engaged as they were in one of the most dangerous professions known to man, sailors tried to improve their chances of success and survival by borrowing what assistance they could from occult forces. Thus it was that Vineyard seamen, before a voyage, took to buying charms from a sorceress who dwelled in the woods of Scrubby Neck on the West Tisbury shore.

It should be noted that, while the witchcraft trials in Salem had occurred over one hundred years before, no one in New England could hang out a shingle as a witch with full immunity from the law and the lynch mobs. The fact that this island spell caster freely peddled her trinkets without local interference shows the high degree of tolerance Vineyarders have always exhibited toward even the most outrageous and eccentric of their neighbors.

The Scrubby Neck sorceress of this tale ran a brisk business selling charms but, it so happened, a well-known sea captain openly refused to buy into her eighteenth-century protection racket. Furious at this rejection, the lady appeared on the dock on the captain's date of departure and taunted him: "You will see plenty of whales but catch none of them!"

Months later, somewhere in the South Seas Archipelago, the witch's curse held true. The crew had followed one school of whales after another without ironing a single catch. One morning a white bird circled the mast shrieking at the men like a furious fishwife. After hours of this treatment, the crew began to fear the peevish bird was the witch herself in feathery disguise. At last, to appease his men's mounting discomfort and fear, the captain fashioned a bullet from a silver dollar and took aim at the bird. He shot it through the heart. Shrieking loudly, the feathered shrew toppled into the sea. The deed was duly recorded in the ship's log, and, lo and behold, from that day forward, whales were harpooned and harvested for their oil.

Two or three years later when the ship returned to its home port, the men learned the witch had, years earlier, according to an eyewitness, fallen dead in her hut at Scrubby Neck. The date of her death was compared with the killing of the white bird, commemorated in the captain's log. The events had taken place at the same hour on the same day.

The area's oldest tale of the supernatural hails from Chappaquiddick Island. Some time in the early 1700s, the island's sole white settler happened to be out on the beach at Wasque. It was a dark and stormy night, (it's always a dark and stormy night in these antique tales), and, beyond the troubled surf, the outlines of a pirate's ship appeared. A rowboat with a pirate chief at the helm and a crew of men streaked towards land.

Hiding behind a boulder, the witness saw the men alight and, by the reedy glow of a lantern, proceed to dig a trench well above the high-water mark. The job completed, the men lowered a wooden chest into the hole. The chief removed a strange package from the folds of his cape and pitched it into the trench. A silent explosion shook the ground and a flash of light consumed the entire beach for a few moments, illuminating every pebble, shrub, and hill with infrared intensity. When the light died, the pirates filled in the hole and departed for their ship.

Shaken to the core, the settler scuttled home. The following day he bruited his eyewitness account all about Martha's Vineyard. For years search teams scoured the beaches below the Wasque cliffs in search of pirate treasure. As far as the records show, none was ever found.

The frightened settler could have encountered much worse. Pirates of the New World, more superstitious even than ordinary sailors of the day, were said to have cultivated a gruesome bit of black magic to protect their treasure: often they would bury alive a member of their own party along with the chest of jewels or gold doubloons. This entombed pirate, they believed, would metamorphose into a guardian ghoul. When New Englanders went hunting for treasure, they in turn, forewarned of these ghastly watchdogs, would place themselves under an oath of silence, for a single vocalized syllable, even a whisper, could summon up the ghost of the buried pirate.

Superstitions have abounded on Martha's Vineyard over the past 350 years. Today if you scrape away the paint on antique doors, you'll find an elderly coat of red. Years ago Vineyarders believed that ghosts could not pass through red doors. Accordingly, legions of householders lacquered their entrances in shades of vermilion.

Over the generations, there have been accounts of sightings of headless horsemen, lights in the forest, explorer Bartholomew Gosnold's phantom ship, a ghostly bride who plies the roads around the fishing village of Menemsha, and other ladies in white hitchhiking rides through the air. The variety of ghosts reflects the variety of people and places on Martha's Vineyard. All of us—alive or dead, real, supernatural, or simply imagined—add to the shimmering colors of "this precious stone set in the silver sea."*

*From William Shakespeare, "The Tempest."

About the Author

HOLLY NADLER researched the Vineyard's supernatural character when she developed a popular "Ghosts of Edgartown" tour. She found that her island neighbors were remarkably willing to tell about their encounters with ghosts, and even more stories surfaced as she compiled *Haunted Island*. A freelance author of both nonfiction and fiction, Ms. Nadler has also written for television. In addition, she operates her own island tour business. She and her family live in Oak Bluffs.